BETTER OFF unDEAD

JAMES PRELLER

FEIWEL AND FRIENDS · NEW YORK

A FEIWEL AND FRIENDS BOOK
An imprint of Macmillan Publishing Group, LLC
175 Fifth Avenue, New York, NY 10010

Our books may be purchased in bulk for promotional, educational, or business use. Please contact your local bookseller or the Macmillan Corporate and Premium Sales Department at (800) 221-7945 ext. 5442 or by e-mail at MacmillanSpecialMarkets@macmillan.com.

Library of Congress Cataloging-in-Publication Data

Names: Preller, James, author.
Title: Better off undead / by James Preller.
Description: First edition. | New York : Feiwel and Friends, 2017. | Summary: Adrian Lazarus,
    who became a zombie just before starting middle school, and new friends Gia, Zander, and
    Talal, navigate a mystery involving global warming, disappearing bees, and billionaire
    developers.
Identifiers: LCCN 2016058773 (print) | LCCN 2017029143 (ebook) |
    ISBN 9781250066480 (hardcover) | ISBN 9781250066497 (ebook)
Subjects: | CYAC: Zombies—Fiction. | Middle schools—Fiction. | Schools—Fiction. |
    Bees—Fiction. | Environmental protection—Fiction. | Adventure and adventurers—
    Fiction. | Mystery and detective stories.
Classification: LCC PZ7.P915 (ebook) | LCC PZ7.P915 Bet 2017 (print) | DDC [Fic]—dc23
LC record available at https://lccn.loc.gov/2016058773

Book design by Carol Ly

Feiwel and Friends logo designed by Filomena Tuosto

First edition, 2017

10 9 8 7 6 5 4 3 2 1

mackids.com

This book is dedicated to the young people
who would like to change the world.
Remember these words of Margaret Mead:
"Never doubt that a small group of thoughtful,
committed citizens can change the world;
indeed, it's the only thing that ever has."

WHAT A WORLD, WHAT A WORLD!

—THE WICKED WITCH OF THE WEST
IN *THE WIZARD OF OZ*

**THERE IS A CRACK IN EVERYTHING.
THAT'S HOW THE LIGHT GETS IN.**

—LEONARD COHEN, "ANTHEM"

SOMETIME IN THE
NOT-SO-DISTANT FUTURE...

MIRROR, MIRROR

Mirror, mirror, on the wall. Who's the deadest of them all?

There I was, lying on my bed on another sticky summer afternoon, examining my reflection in a hand mirror. I pondered the first day of seventh grade, just four days away, and gazed at my decomposing face.

It wasn't too bad, considering I was dead. When you took into account that minor detail and then compared me to all the other dead people in the world, hey, I was doing all right. Better than all right!

Go ahead: Dig up a grave, stick the corpse in a wicker chair next to me, and then compare and contrast. Do a Venn diagram for all I care. I'll win that beauty contest eight days a week, twice on Sunday.

That's me, Adrian Lazarus: way hotter than most dead people.

Compared to living folks, the ones who aren't full-on zombies, maybe I don't look so great. Mine is a face only a mother could love, though I was beginning to have my doubts about that. After all, how could she? The whole zombie thing had been tough on Mom. She hadn't bargained for a zombie with bad breath, body odor, and a hunger for braaaaains. Just kidding about the dietary issues. I'm pretty satisfied with an undercooked hamburger and greasy fries. Not super hungry these days.

A fly touched down on the windowsill near my bare feet. It lifted off again like a barnstorming pilot, performed a few dives, loop-the-loops, and barrel rolls over my exposed flesh. It buzzed my face before squeezing out a hole in the window screen. Probably just an advance scout for the coming swarm. It would tell the other flies they hit the jackpot.

That's one of the downsides of zombie life. Ha, there's a phrase, *zombie life*: an oxymoron, like *plastic glass* and *jumbo shrimp* and *cafeteria food*. I attract flies. They follow me in black clouds like I'm the Pied Piper. Kneel down before me, for I am the true Lord of the Flies!

I was basking in my misery when the door opened. As usual, my little brother, Dane, was itching to enter my inner sanctum. As if the closed door meant nothing, and the words KEEP OUT! signaled an open invitation. Dane poked his chubby-cheeked, pug-nosed face into the room. His head was seemingly squished from forehead to chin so that it resembled an old, soft orange. To me, Dane's smooth, dark, elastic cheeks made him look like a living garden gnome, hideous and adorable at the same time.

Dane was four years old. And unlike his big brother, very much alive.

"Hi," Dane said. "What are you doing?"

I was doing exactly nothing, but I told him I was reading a comic book. A believable lie, since I often flipped through comic books and graphic novels.

There were a few comics scattered by my pillow. Reading was doing something, a way of being alone and yet totally (amazingly) connected to something else, some faraway place called anywhere but here, which is where I longed to be. Without turning around, I grabbed a comic book and held it up for Dane.

"See," I said, swiveling my head, back still to him.

"The Sandman," Dane murmured with awe. He stepped into the room, emboldened. Dane wore red shorts held up by an elastic waistband. He had on his favorite T-shirt—the one with a picture of the Scarecrow from *The Wizard of Oz*. Inspired by his favorite movie character, Dane often stumbled around the house, pratfalling like the boneless, brainless man of straw, windmilling his stubby arms, humming the tune from the movie.

If I only had a brain.

Concern creased Dane's face. "Can I come in?" he asked, already in.

I shrugged. All I wanted was to be left alone. But Dane needed to be near, I knew. Even a dope like me can see when he's loved. It's better than nothing, by a lot.

"Where's Mom? Yoga class? Work?" I asked.

"She's on the phone, talking to somebody about periodic rate caps," Dane explained, without a flicker of comprehension as to what he was saying. He could join the club. I didn't know what periodic rate caps were, either. That was Mom's work. Flipping houses, skimming a percentage off the top, moving on like a shark in bloody waters. Buying and selling.

After my father went overseas with Corporate to fight in the Water Wars, and kept reenlisting, Mom reinvented herself. Today she's a successful real estate agent. I couldn't walk three blocks in town without seeing her face beaming out from a FOR SALE sign: ROSIE LAZARUS, AN AGENT YOU CAN TRUST.

Dane reached into his pocket and produced two sour-apple candies. My little brother knew the way to my heart—through the gap in my rotten teeth and down into the cavities. He offered both to me.

I took one, told him to keep one for himself, pulled on the twisted ends of the crinkly wrapper, and popped the hard candy into my mouth. I grunted "thanks" and returned to my horrible mirror.

I sighed. "I might run away." I could see Dane standing behind me now, reflected in the mirror, pressing closer. I felt his sticky fingers on my back, heard the hard candy rattling against his teeth.

"Don't go to California, it's on fire," Dane said.

After years of drought, wildfires had started up and kept spreading. Nobody was running away to California anymore. "Not all of it," I said.

"Oh," he said, blinking. Dane considered the news in silence. "Can I have your room?"

"Dane!"

His head pivoted on his shoulders as he eyed the walls and sloped ceiling, redecorating in his imagination. He'd probably fill it with Legos. Dane caught my eye in the mirror's reflection. "Mom would be mad if you ran away."

Maybe mad, I thought. *Or relieved.* "You hungry?"

The sweet boy with fat cheeks and loose curls nodded. Yes, he was hungry. Dane was always hungry.

I sat up and put my feet on the carpet for the first time in hours. My toes were numb, like dull weights, lead sinkers on a fishing line. No nerve endings. I could take an ax and chop them off, from big toe to little toe, and never feel a thing. Pop 'em off like grapes from the stem.

Dane took my cold, clammy hand. "Come," he said, and tugged, dragging me from my dark room into the light.

HOW I DIED

I guess you'd like to know how I died. That's the first question anybody asks a zombie. Don't feel bad, it's only natural. People are curious creatures, like ferrets or cats or whatever. I don't know—I'm not an animal expert.

"How'd you die?" they ask, leaning in a little, eager for the gory details. They hope to hear about a horrendous, bone-crunching accident with a wood chipper. The bloodier, the better. But I'm like: Seriously? Enough already. I'm dead. A medical marvel, a deviation from the norm, the world's ultimate outsider. Aren't the facts enough? Now I've got to entertain you with bloody stories, too?

Well, sorry to disappoint. How I died isn't all that dramatic. What I really want to tell you is how I survived. Seventh grade, that is. Plus the unraveling planet, I guess. You know, the superflu and diminishing species, the melting ice caps and rising seas, the killer wasps and strangled lakes. But, okay, enough of that. First let's get the death-and-reanimated-corpse stuff out of the way.

I don't mean to get super sensitive about it, but I've got feelings, too, even if my nerve endings don't fire correctly. I'm not a carnival sideshow freak performing for your entertainment. Here's the deal: I was on my bike, sneezing from a pollen attack, when I took a sloppy turn around a corner and got hit by some random car moving too fast. I flew twenty feet in the air, cartwheeling head over shoe, and landed like a sack of laundry. Lights out. No, I wasn't wearing a helmet at the time—and you can spare me the lecture. I know. Believe me, I know. I'd like to say that I learned my lesson and now, like a good citizen, wear a helmet everywhere I go, but that's not true. I'm already dead, so it's not like a little head trauma's going to do much damage. You want to rekill a zombie, you're going to have to do better than that. It requires a precise, powerful blow to the—wait. I'm not telling you.

That's another curious aspect to my condition. Zombies do not want to get killed a second time. You might assume that we wouldn't care. But it's not true. By the way, you might notice that I write *we* when speaking of zombies, plural. That's just a wild guess. Or maybe a faint hope. For the record, I have no proof that there are other zombies. I might be the only one. A true one-of-a-kind original. I've come to realize something about people: No matter who they are, no matter what their lives are like, everybody wants to hold on to what they've got—even if it's nothing much. Even the guy shivering in a cardboard box under the train tracks, or the grandmother clinging to life support in a hospital oxygen tent. We're all grateful for each gasp of breath, despite everything.

Everybody knows it really could be worse.

Even a zombie like me.

(Later on, it was math with Mrs. Chen that nearly did me in, bored to death while I tried to solve inequalities in one variable. My answer to math is: What difference does it make to the rest of my life on the planet?)

As for why I reanimated, sitting up in the ambulance with a panicked jolt, nobody knows. Stuff happens. I didn't even realize that I was dead at first, but it became obvious by the way the EMTs reared away from me as if they'd seen a ghost.

No, jerkwads, not a ghost. A zombie, yes; but not a ghost. Ack, thud. We almost needed to call an ambulance . . . for the ambulance!

That was the first hint I wasn't alive anymore. Blood no longer pumped through my veins. No heartbeat. I was as undead as a toenail, and not really thrilled about it.

Needless to say, my parents freaked, but there, I already said it. They're still married but worlds apart—Dad has so moved on, deployed in Africa, a mercenary soldier working for Corporate—but for this they came together via the Interwebs for a few troublesome, confusing days. You could say I'm a disappointment to my parents. Sour-faced, pulsing with pimples, my skin black and blue, an inconvenient monster.

My body wasn't too messed up in the accident. It was a clean kill, as the local bow hunters like to say. Some internal bleeding, a bump on the noggin, and a broken ankle that still gives me trouble. I'm a cliché that way, the foot-dragging zombie, limping along.

I don't have many friends. But you guessed that, right? I mean, I have precisely one: Zander. His full name is Zander Donnelly, and he is so out there, so deep into his own weird zone, I don't think he even realized I had crossed over to the realm of the undead. The great thing about Zander is, I don't think he'd care either way.

DRINK PLENTY
OF FLUIDS

I was a busy guy during the first week of my death. Sort of the opposite of what you'd imagine, right? You'd assume it would be quiet, even relaxing, being dead and all. But not in my unlife. There was a lot to do.

For the first few days after the accident, I was seen by every medical expert in the area, even people from the FBI and mysterious others flashing U.S. government badges. All day long they wandered into my hospital room to marvel at the new patient. They looked at me and frowned, clucked and murmured, and said helpful things like, "Hmmm, interesting, interesting." I was a fascinating case, a puzzlement. I was tested, probed, poked, prodded, scanned, questioned, measured, charted, and MRI'd until, finally, the folks in their white coats shrugged with a mixture of defeat and boredom. After three sleep-interrupted nights of liquids dripping and machines beeping, I was told to go home. Something about insurance costs. There was nothing to be done. After that, I was assigned to the primary care of Dr. Noah Halpert. He was some hotshot specialist flown in from who-knows-where. And so we visited his pristine office for regular checkups at the K & K MediCorp building. As far as I could tell, I was his only patient.

On the day when my bad news got worse, I played with the controls of a leatherette recliner of the type normally found in a dentist's office. My mother fiddled with her new watch computer, setting up the connection with my dad, who was still deployed at an unspecified location somewhere on the African continent. Dad couldn't give us details on his work assignments—it was hush-hush—and we'd often go months without a word. Even so, he was supportive about my situation. Dad said he wanted to come home immediately, but, well, the Corporation couldn't let him go just yet. He was a second lieutenant in a privatized army outsourced by the government, and Corporate depended on him. Skype was Dad's way of being there, a grim-faced, square-jawed head on a computer screen.

The room was filled with glass surfaces and glittering utensils. I kept catching my reflection staring at the strange surroundings like a startled woodland creature. Chapped-lipped, sore-faced, hideous: zombic mc. I missed the identity of my dark skin in our mostly white town. I used to be the black kid, but not anymore. Race, religion, politics—"zombie" trumped them all. After another routine examination—reflexes, none; eyesight, failing; sense of smell, gone; etc.—Dr. Halpert looked at me, his mustache drooping and his eyes flickering with indecision. He parked heavily on a stool and rolled close to me, leaning in. "Adrian," he began, raising his palms as a sign of surrender. "As doctors, we like to think we have all the answers. We possess all this expensive equipment, years of scientific research . . ." His voice trailed off, losing steam. He sighed, checked my mother with a glance, looked hopelessly at my father's image on the laptop screen. "But there's so much we don't know. That's just a fact."

I watched him, gave a nod. At least he was honest.

"By every measure we currently employ, medically speaking, you should be dead," Dr. Halpert said.

My throat felt dry. My tongue seemed to swell. I tried to swallow.

"You don't have a heartbeat," Dr. Halpert stated. "Yet here we are. We have tested you in every conceivable manner. And the fact is"—he ran his thumb and index finger down his thick mustache—"the fact is . . ." He repeated himself, struggling to find the words. "We just . . . don't . . . know . . . diddly."

"But, Doctor—" my mother interjected.

"Oh, we have theories. We could sit around and speculate all day long. It might be this, it might be that. An exotic strain of virus. Ebola this, superflu that, cancer-causing agents in the water table, the fallout from fracking, too many genetically engineered foods, a new strain of dengue fever, or just plain bad luck. All I know, Adrian, is that you are—"

"A freak," I said.

"No, no, no," Dr. Halpert said. "A miracle! And as a man of science, it kills me to say that. I don't believe in miracles, Adrian. I believe in facts, hard data, research. We simply don't understand how you are walking around today, much less why. Talking. Seeing. Thinking. And, seemingly, living. It makes no scientific sense. When it comes to your case, Adrian, we might as well be in the Dark Ages, applying leeches and burning incense."

"Is it . . . contagious?" asked my mother, inching away ever so slightly.

"Not at all," the doctor replied. "It's certainly not an airborne virus or anything of that nature. Of course, I wouldn't let him bite you, ha-ha-ha!" He turned to me, smiling broadly. "You're not going to bite your mother, are you, Adrian? Of course not!"

I joked, "Yeah, no, I just had a big lunch."

More laughter, *ho-ho-ho*, even my dad thought it was a laugh riot. Mom, however, didn't seem amused. Her mouth laughed, but her eyes didn't get the joke. Mom's cell buzzed with an incoming message. She checked it, frowned. She was missing work for this appointment.

Dr. Halpert looked at me and waited. I didn't know what to say. I rarely did. My thoughts refused to organize themselves; the words wouldn't cohere. My mind was a buzz, a beehive, a blur, a whir. I stared at him, blinking, thinking, coming up empty.

My father broke the silence. "Well, that's not a very satisfactory answer, is it, Doctor?"

Dr. Halpert shook his head. "No, it isn't," he admitted.

"So what now?" my father asked.

Dr. Halpert glanced at me and then back to the computer image of his inquisitor. "Summer's almost over. School starts in another week or so. Middle school, I guess."

"You think he can go to school?" my mother chimed in, shock registering in her voice. "You think it's all right?"

"Life goes on," the doctor replied. He scratched his cheek with nervous fingers, tugged at his white lab coat. Perhaps Dr. Halpert recognized the irony of his own words—this crazy situation—so he quickly added, "I mean, Mr. and Mrs. Lazarus, I don't see the harm in it. Admittedly, Adrian's is an unusual case. Bizarre, truly. No one has an explanation for what's happened to your son. By everything we know, there's simply no way on earth your boy should be sitting in my office having this conversation. There's no heartbeat! He's dried up, blood doesn't course through his arteries. He's a zom—"

The doctor stopped himself, embarrassed or unwilling to finish the word; so it hung in the air, unspoken, like a bubble on the verge of bursting. *Zombie.* I felt a twitch in my stomach. If I had anything to hurl, I would have upchucked right there on the floor.

The thought of starting seventh grade made my head spin.

My mother sat staring at me, the downward turn of a frown on her lips. She made a dabbing gesture on her face, as if applying phantom makeup. "Is there anything we can do to . . . ?"

"Ah yes! I almost forgot," Dr. Halpert said, jumping out of his seat cheerfully. He pulled open a cabinet door, then another, reached for bottles, pushed others aside, scanned labels. By the time he was finished, the counter was cluttered with all sorts of medicines and potions. "The good news is, there are some very simple things we can do to stave off the symptoms."

The doctor read the question in my eyes.

"I don't think we can cure you, Adrian—this is uncharted territory for all of us—but there's a lot we can do to keep the, urm, illness from progressing. You know, just by using standard over-the-counter products such as creams, lotions, eye drops, salves, and whatnot. ChapStick, for example, works wonders," Dr. Halpert said. "And drinking plenty of fluids will help, too."

My mother listened intently, obviously interested. She finally had something to latch on to after days of helpless hoping. They weren't going to try to cure my condition. Nope, they just wanted to conceal it.

"Essentially, Adrian, you've lost your vital secretions. Your body is drying up, no juices, and we can't have that."

"I see," my mother murmured, grasping the concept. She said, "It's like putting on hand moisturizer. I do that every night before bed, Adrian." She raised her smooth, well-moisturized hands as if they were exhibits in a legal proceeding.

I smiled weakly.

"Exactly," Dr. Halpert chirped. "We've got to keep him . . . squishy."

Both of them chuckled over the word. *Squishy.* Ho-ho. Meanwhile, I scratched at the skin on my dry, flaking knees. "Doctor," I spoke up. "I don't have a heartbeat. My face is falling apart—my face! Are you seriously telling me to drink lots of water?"

He shook his head. "No, no, no. I mean, yes . . . and no. The truth is, Adrian, water will help. Lots of it. A gallon a day, maybe two in your case. But I have something else in mind, too." He plucked a pink pad from his front coat pocket, scribbled on it, tore off the top sheet, and handed it to my mother.

She scanned it and read, " 'Formaldehyde smoothies'?"

"Formaldehyde is a common embalming agent," Dr. Halpert explained. "It's frequently used in, urm,"—he gestured with his hand, pulled again on his thick mustache, and went on in a muffled voice— "funeral homes and whatnot." *Cough cough.*

"On dead bodies?" I asked.

My mother gaped at me, neck stretched forward, as if to say, *Don't be rude.* I felt pressure behind my eyes, a welling up, but no tears came. Not squishy enough, I guess. No juices. Real zombies don't cry.

The doctor continued. "Formaldehyde helps preserve dead tissue—though it's most often used as a fixative for microscopy and histology, but never mind that. The point is, Adrian, if you drink one of these smoothies every morning, I believe it will help keep you looking better, feeling better, and, urm, smelling fresher."

He stood to open a window.

For a moment I thought about jumping out of it. But what would be the point?

Dead was bad. Middle school would be worse.

OUR SUPER-NORMAL DINNER

Things got pretty weird around my house in the daze between the appointment at Dr. Halpert's office and the first day of school. And by "pretty weird," I mean totally awkward and miserable. I watched as my mother came to grips with the reality of my predicament. Her adjustment involved a lot of Kleenex and bad television. If I overheard another television commercial for Pretty Pillz, I was going to lose it. At the beginning, my mother kept asking why, why, why, as if there was some reasonable explanation why this thing had happened to her child. I didn't have time for questions like that. Boy becomes zombie because . . . because . . . just because, that's why. Not everything in the world has to make sense. Watch the news on TV and you'll know it's true.

I found myself thinking about wood-witted, heavy-footed Pinocchio in his feathered cap and dumb red shorts. All he wanted was to become a real boy. A living, breathing one of the dudes. We shared that deepest dream, Pinocchio and I, to hear our caged hearts quicken beneath our ribs, *pitter-pat, pitter-pat*, like little cat paws scampering across wooden floors.

I wanted to live, to be a real boy.

My mother tried her best. I felt sorry for her. Everything she did only made it worse. She tried to make everything so . . . bizarrely . . . normal. For example, on the night before the first day of school, she came home from work extra peppy, like she was a walking, talking glass of ginger ale. Mom rolled up her sleeves and plunged into the kitchen, frantically cutting vegetables, stir-frying a big mound of chopped beef, heating taco shells in the oven until their consistency was the perfect crispness. Mom knew it used to be my favorite dinner, and tonight was going to be magical in every way. Just me, my mother, and Dane sitting around the table. One small happy family—as long as we ignored the facts that, well, gee, Adrian is a zombie and, oh yeah, Dad is in some far-flung war over the earth's last valuable resource: safe, clean water. Other than that, hey, these tacos are delicious.

I wasn't hungry. I seemed to have lost my taste for food. But I forced down a taco for Mom's sake. She chattered nervously—about work, about the crazy weather, about the state of the housing market; celebrity marriages, makeover shows, sporting events, oil spills, and windmills. Like a dork, I spilled a big glass of soda. My clumsy undead digits were about as handy as bowling pins. *Zing!* My mother leaped out of her chair with a wild look in her eyes, like it really, really freaked her out, this spilled-soda thing. She cried in a too loud, too tense voice, "EVERYBODY BACK! NOBODY MOVE! I'VE GOT IT! THIS IS NOT A PROBLEM!"

Dane and I exchanged glances. Mom hurried to the sink and ran water through the filtration system. I watched her shoulders heave up and down, up and down, trembling, and I knew she was losing it. I really felt bad for her right then, and ashamed, because it was my fault. Why couldn't I be a normal kid? Dane, ever wise, whispered to me, "Don't watch," and crunched into his taco. We waited with our heads down while our mother, twelve feet away, tried to pull herself together. Finally she turned to us with a big, desperate smile plastered across her splotchy face. "Let's make tonight Family Game Night!" she announced. "We never play games anymore. We used to, don't you remember? Adrian? Dane? Remember how we used to play games, and Daddy was here, and it was so much fun—just so much fun?"

I looked at Dane, unsure if she'd asked a

question-question or one of those fake questions that you aren't supposed to answer. I thought, *Maybe school won't be so bad after all.* Comparatively.

Turns out I was wrong about that.

MIDDLE SCHOOL BLUES

The doors to Nixon Middle School opened on a hot September day. I felt like a deer out for a stroll on opening day of hunting season. Students poured into the building, a liquid stream of sixth, seventh, and eighth graders. Most wore shorts, except for me and a few assorted misfits. I'd covered up as much of my body as I could, so instead I baked in the heat of stiff new jeans and a long-sleeve, waffle-knit shirt. There was nothing I could do to hide my face, though I was tempted to throw a sack over my head. But I figured if girls weren't allowed to wear spaghetti-strap shirts, then I wasn't going to be able to walk around with a bag over my head. I opted for a hoodie instead.

My face had become the accident on the side of the road. I caused traffic jams and pileups just by walking down the hallway. Everybody slowed down to gawk at my unsightly mug. They stared with fascination and disgust, unwilling to pass without a good gander. Classmates craned their necks to see. The sixth graders, new to middle school, gazed with worried glances, careful to make it appear they weren't staring at all. Whereas eighth graders were bolder. They looked at me in bug-eyed disbelief, frowning as if my presence somehow ruined their perfect day.

That's when the comments began, whispered from behind my back: *shuffler, drooler, cadaver, freak.* I had to get away, so I gimped into the boys' room.

The bathroom was empty and echoing; the uneven clomp of my heavy heels bounced off tiled walls. I assessed myself in the cloudy mirror. And for that one second, I wasn't any different from every other student in seventh grade. We all looked at ourselves a lot, frowning, rearranging unruly hair, tugging on our shirts, distraught over a new zit. I stood and stared. No wonder nobody wanted to look at me. I didn't even want to see it—and it was *my own face*! But I guess I should paint you a picture, right? Isn't that what all the supposedly terrific writers do? They go on and on about what characters wear, endless descriptions of furniture and clothing accessories that most readers (like me) skip past, searching for the good parts.

I'll be quick about it, promise.

I wore my hair exactly the same way as before, long with a loose, natural flow. I sometimes twisted the ends of random sections to give it extra wow. Not bad, and definitely not my main problem. Besides my fingernails, my hair was the only part of my body that was still growing, so I wasn't about to cut it. My eyes were smallish and sunken, with dark shadows underneath. I looked dead tired. Lips: Yep, still had 'em, but there was a large cold sore in one corner, cracked and chapped, that no amount of lip balm could solve. My skin had turned from brown to a shade of gray, tinged with green. The terrain of my cheeks was rough, pocked with red explosions, black marks, and flaking patches. Maybe I just needed a good dermatologist, like every other kid in school, or a year's supply of Pretty Pillz.

I looked in the mirror and thought, *That's not me. That's not who I really am.*

ZANDER DONNELLY

Fifth-period lunch, not even hungry. The smell from last school year lingered on, amazingly, strong enough to reach even my faulty senses. Odors clung to the walls, emanated from waxed floors, and filtered lazily through the school ventilation system. Middle school's pungent bouquet, as if summer, with its soft breezes and green grass, had never been. My nostrils filled with a witch's brew of sweat, raspberry-scented lip gloss, mysterious meatballs, soggy pizza, and cleaning fluids. I found a small table in a corner and waited for some of last year's regulars to join me. Nobody did.

Except for Zander.

I noticed that his shirt was on backward, and inside out, too. Zander wasn't real sharp with personal maintenance. I hadn't seen him in weeks, not since the accident, but nothing much had changed. Same pasty skin, rumpled clothing, and doughy body. Zander glanced in my direction, not quite meeting my eyes. He nodded once and stared gloomily at his cardboard lunch tray. Besides the apple he wouldn't eat and the milk carton he wouldn't open, Zander had opted for the bean-and-cheese burrito special.

He muttered something about the "stupid healthy-meals initiative."

"What?"

"I'd like to see the government get out of my Cheetos," he griped.

I watched in silence as Zander unfolded his burrito for inspection. He moved cautiously, beads of sweat forming on his forehead, like a hero in an action movie about to dismantle a bomb. Should he cut the red wire or the green? Zander stabbed at the inner brown muck with a plastic spork, sniffed, and pushed the tray aside. A sigh escaped from his lips.

I slid my unnecessary tuna fish sandwich across the table as an offering of friendship. He took it, murmured "thanks," pulled the crust off with his fingers, and nibbled at the sandwich. As we tentatively talked about our classes and teachers, the distance melted away and our natural friendship took hold. We were scheduled for only one class together, with a new science teacher named Ms. Fjord, who had already displayed an alarming, bright-eyed eagerness. I wondered if maybe she was a little too *into* it. Zander sat with his shoulders hunched by his ears, eyes scanning the crowded lunchroom. He leaned in. "I want you to know, Adrian, I heard about what happened," he said in a low whisper, careful not to be overheard. "That's so messed up."

"You heard?"

"There's been a lot of talk, texts and stuff," he said.

"What have you heard?" I asked.

Zander looked away. He couldn't bring himself

to say it. I knew then that he'd heard the truth—and probably worse.

"You got my text, right?" he asked. "I wanted to come over, but my parents—"

"It's okay," I said.

"They were like—"

"It's okay," I repeated, a little louder this time, shutting him off like a bad song on the radio. He looked hurt. I shrugged. "People are afraid, I guess." I looked around the lunchroom. It was true. Old classmates sat across the room, backs turned. Worse, some stole sly glances in my direction, distrust on their faces. They were frightened, all of them, and they hated me for it. The air was thick with it.

I was an outcast.

"You going to eat those chips?" Zander asked. I blinked, stirred out of my reverie by his question. Poof, like that, the atmosphere changed. Zander didn't care. I gladly handed him my potato chips. Took a sip from my thermos, frowned. It tasted like medicine.

"What's that?" Zander asked.

I told him about my formaldehyde smoothie.

"Now that I'm dead, my mom's gone health nut on me."

Zander laughed, a surprised chortle. "You seem pretty cool about this whole . . . change."

I shrugged. "Sucks to be me. But what am I gonna do?"

"Could you sue the guy who hit you?"

"Hit and run," I said. "Never saw the driver's face, barely saw the car. It happened fast. One minute I was on my bike; next minute I was flying through the air like a circus acrobat. No net, no witnesses." I paused, hoping to change the subject. "What you been up to?"

"I got some new fish. A leopard shark and a firefish," he said, brightening. Zander loved his aquarium. He was a dedicated hobbyist, obsessed with his saltwater tank, a forty-gallon behemoth that dominated his bedroom. The setup was pretty impressive, actually, with cool lights and bubbles, a tank he kept immaculate and filled with interesting-looking fish, rocks, and coral. And by "interesting-looking," I mean pretty cool for about two minutes. Zander could watch his fish for hours at a time, and I'm sure that's what he did each day, beanbag chair pulled up close. He cleaned the glass daily with Windex and paper towels.

"I'd love to see 'em," I lied.

Zander chewed his lower lip, and I could tell that an invite to his house wasn't in the cards. He said, "I guess the big thing from this summer is, um, I'm worried about the honeybees."

"Did you just say, 'I'm worried about the honeybees'?"

Zander confirmed that was exactly what he'd said. "Rising carbon levels, that's a problem. The ice caps melting. Dying coral reefs. Robot drones dropping bombs. And then there's the genetic engineering of food—the other day I saw a strawberry the size of my head!—but who doesn't stress out over that?"

"Actually, most people don't," I said. "Why are you worried about honeybees?"

Zander smirked. "Just bee-cause. Get it? Bee-cause? Because. Bee-cause!"

"Really?" I said, shaking my head. "That's your joke? I can't bee-lieve you just said that."

Zander giggled and crunched down on a stack of chips. "Don't you read?" he said. "The honeybees are disappearing."

It rang a distant gong in my cranium. "Maybe I remember seeing something about it on TV."

"Scientists call it a die-off, or if you want to get technical, colony collapse disorder," Zander informed me. "All the worker bees just suddenly vanish. They don't even find dead bodies. It's like aliens abducted them or something."

"Get out," I said.

"No, it's happening all over the world. In Europe—places like Belgium, France, Spain. In Taiwan. And now it's here in North America."

"So is this, like, a problem?" I asked.

"It's a huge problem. Honeybees are pollinators. They do good things for the environment, for farmers and stuff. They pollinate crops, keep things in balance. Farms need bees, people need farms. But now entire populations are getting wiped out all over the world. It's like nature's not natural anymore."

"That's bizarre," I said, actually interested. "Does anybody know why?"

Zander explained that scientists had a bunch of theories, though no one knew for sure. "Pesticides, probably. I was talking to Ms. Fjord after class today—"

"Wait a minute," I interrupted. "You talked to a teacher . . . after the first day of class?"

"Yeah, briefly." Zander nodded. "She's all right. I might help her out with the hive this year. She's a beekeeper, you know, and she's installing a hive by the organic garden out back. We might even start a bee club."

"Glee club?"

"Bee club," he said.

"Hmmm," I deadpanned. "So that's what the buzz was about."

Zander paid no mind to the pun. He told me, "Ms. Fjord says these big, billion-dollar chemical corporations get farmers to use freaky chemicals—called neonics—to treat seeds. But they act like a poison to the bees that come to collect pollen."

Zander grew stressed just talking about it. I could hear the eagerness in his voice. Sure, Zander was always an excitable guy. It wasn't new to hear him talk about endangered species like lowland gorillas or black rhinos or humpback whales. But bees? He sounded really, really into it this time.

"You know what's crazy?" he said. "Supposedly they use these chemicals to protect the crops from destructive insects, but those chemicals are killing the bees—and the farmers need the bees to grow the crops. It's mad stupid."

"And we're, like, screwed?" I asked.

"Yep," Zander agreed. "It's not good for anybody, but it's really bad for the bees."

"So you want to work with Ms. Fjord's honey-bees," I said.

"Yeah," Zander replied. "It won't change the world, but it might, you know, change the world . . . a little bit."

"It's better than nothing," I said.

"That's what I think," Zander agreed, chomping on my final chip.

TROUBLE IN P.E.

I sat on the bench in front of my gym locker. The guys from class moved around, got undressed, dressed, tossed balled-up shirts and pants into small lockers, slammed the metal doors shut, joked and blustered, talked sports, complained about teachers, and, finally, hustled out the door. They all accomplished this while avoiding looking directly at each other's semi-undressed bodies.

Even non-zombies, I realized, felt uncomfortable in their own skin.

At last, I was alone. Or nearly alone. I sensed a

few others in the row of lockers behind me, heard them talking in whispers. Footsteps came closer, and Daryl Northrup sat on the bench beside me. There was plenty of room, tons of it, but he sidled up too close. I sat still, unmoving, my hands on my lap, waiting for him to go away. Daryl wasn't a guy I wanted to cross.

"Yo, Adrian!" Daryl said, his voice about three notches above cheerful. The tone was false, a lie.

I didn't reply. Daryl wasn't a "How ya doing?" kind of guy. In fact, this was the first time he'd ever spoken to me. I mostly tried to avoid guys like Daryl Northrup. I studied the tile floor. Daryl sniffed in an exaggerated way, the way a three-year-old might noisily sniff a flower. "Stinks in here, don't it?" he commented. "I mean, crap, it's totally disgusting."

I heard laughter from behind me. Daryl was talking to me, but not really talking to me at all. It was a one-man performance put on for a faceless audience snickering behind the row of lockers. I glanced at my combination lock. I could spin the dial, yank it open, ignore him. Instead, my nervous fingers clutched at the bottom of my shirt. I made an effort to press my hands against my thighs, the way a relaxed person might.

Daryl kept talking. "It smells like something died in here, you know what I'm saying? Like a rat ate some poison, then crawled into the walls and died. Do you smell it, Adrian? Because I sure do. Isn't that right? Like a disgusting rat just up and died?"

I didn't say a word. Didn't move a muscle. Instead, I waited. Time would pass, it always does. Things would change, bells would ring, and Daryl Northrup would one day be dead and buried in the ground with worms crawling through his eye sockets. I pictured that in my mind, and it helped me feel a little better.

At times like these, I try to think happy thoughts.

"You know what they should do?" Daryl said to me. "Do you?"

He waited, obviously expecting an answer.

I glanced sideways in his direction. Shook my head. I had no idea what they should do.

"They need to fumigate this place. We've got to

get rid of the disgusting smell around here. It's not fit for humans, don't you think, Adrian? Wouldn't we all be better off if the dead-animal stink was gone completely?"

More laughter rippled from behind me, drifting over the lockers. A door swung open and a voice echoed in the room. Ms. Caputo, our P.E. teacher. "All right, boys. Get a move on! We're headed outside for our track-and-field unit. No excuses, let's go!"

Daryl slowly rose, as though standing up was a big chore. He stood there, towering over me. His open right hand violently shot forward and smashed into a locker, *blam!* The noise thundered and echoed in the room. If my heart had been functional, it would have skipped a beat. Instead, I sat there, calm as a clam, waiting for this to end.

For it all to end.

"We need to get rid of these rats, that's what I say!" Daryl sputtered, and he skulked past me.

I never left the locker room for class. Just not into it. Health and fitness was another one of those concepts you have to let go of after you die. I was never going to score a touchdown for the home team. The cheerleaders were never going to spell out my name. In horror, maybe, but never with pride. So I hung out by my lonesome, counting tiles, wondering if I could maybe ask for a note from Dr. Halpert: *Please excuse Adrian Lazarus from P.E. on account of the fact he's dead.*

STICKS AND STONES

Let's list the names:

I am shuffler, ankle-dragger, shape-shifter, howler, freak. I am living dead, soulless corpse, brain-sucker, crawler, spitter, wraith, wuss, dumb butt, flailer, mutant, hant. I am gorgon, raver, basilisk, shambling undead, moaner, groaner, ghoul, death talker, puke machine, shade, half-life, cadaver, wailer, flailer, biter, roamer, feeder, lurcher, loser, infected fleshbag, vermin, oddball, slob, dipstick, drooler, death rattler, human fail.

I am other, alien, outcast, misfit, and I live in your town.

I am zombie, and names will never hurt me.

But inside, I'm a flower rising up through a crack in the sidewalk. I'm a hawk riding the upswells of wind, an athlete leaping hurdles, heart pumping, blood pulsing . . .

Inside, in the places that no one can see, I'm freaking amazing.

THE GIRL WHO
COULD READ MINDS

And so it went. I dragged myself up and down the
hallways, into classrooms, through days and weeks.
I drank three formaldehyde shakes a day. Applied
the creams, administered the eye drops. My out-
ward appearance didn't get any better, but it didn't
get much worse. At least my limbs weren't falling
off. My mom experimented with different flavors
for the shakes, and I liked green-berry best. Otherwise, my appetite had all but disappeared, which

was definitely . . . weird. I was living on Airheads, Laffy Taffy, and whatever other candy Zander shared with me. He was a sugar addict and had maybe the worst diet in the world. Zander claimed candy was safer than the fake food produced in the big, corporate farm factories. "Genetically modified organisms," he said ominously. "GMOs. Who knows what that stuff does to you? I don't want to be some corporation's human guinea pig."

I was like, shrug, *I guess.*

At home, things weren't terrible. My mother had normalized to her routine of showing houses, meeting clients, negotiating deals, and chasing big bucks. Plus, she was meditating more than ever. I wondered if she hoped to levitate someday. Anyway, Mom was too busy to give us grief. Dane went to preschool happily, and we got along fine, same as always. Most nights, I heated up a frozen pizza for him or ordered takeout from the Chinese place. Dane was crazy for chicken lo mein, fortune cookies, and cans of soda. He constantly stuffed his chubby little munchkin face with Cheez-Its. The truth is, I liked my kid brother a lot. Besides Zander,

Dane was the one person who treated me the same as always. I guess he needed a big brother, dead or alive.

School was a different story. I was worse than unpopular. I was now an afterthought, an absence, a black hole in the universe. I was invisible except for the times when I appeared as a target for the creeps, like a duck in a shooting gallery. Here's a quick story, about the first time I met Gia Demeter.

On Tuesdays, I had exactly four minutes to get from math to band class, which was way on the other side of the building. I navigated through crowded hallways, plodded down a flight of stairs on my bad ankle, and stopped at my locker. I fumbled with the dial, twiddling like a lunatic. Dry patches of skin flaked off my fingers. Time was ticking and I still had to reach the darkest, dankest corner of the middle school, where the rented violas and French horns were kept. Not mission impossible, but my assignment left no time for lollygagging (not that I lollygagged, because who does, really).

Mr. Steel, my music teacher, was clear: "I do not tolerate lateness," he informed the class. Every time somebody came in after the bell, he did a pantomime of crossing his arms, shutting his mouth mid-sentence, and staring at that person with laser-beam eyeballs until the student took a seat. Mr. Steel wanted you to know that he thought you were the lowest thing on earth—a bug, a worm—just for coming in two minutes late.

So I tried to get there on time. And sometimes I made it.

Down the hallway loped predatory Daryl Northrup, shoulders rolling, cool and free. Despite myself, I secretly admired the guy. He was my opposite. The alpha dog, leader of the pack, not a worry in the world—and I stupidly made the mistake of making eye contact.

Daryl's expression changed immediately. Without breaking stride, he lowered his shoulder, gave me a hard bump into the locker, and said from the corner of his mouth, "Get a life, zombie boy."

Great advice, don't you think? I'll work on that.

But you know what else I thought? This is sort of pathetic, but I'll admit it: I thought, *I wish we could be friends.*

"No, you don't."

I turned to see an extremely tall girl standing beside me. A toothpick with pointy elbows and long legs. Her name was Gia Demeter—that's all I knew about her. Not from around here, new to town. She had lank black hair, a pointy beak, and pale skin. Her hands dangled at her sides like white tarantulas. Gia looked at me through unusually large, round eyes, her head tilted slightly forward. I stepped back, uncomfortable under her green-eyed gaze.

Was she talking to me?

I grumbled a few words about minding your own business, then returned to spinning the dial on the locker. I was seriously going to be late for band class. But for the unlife of me, I couldn't remember my combination.

"That guy," she said, "is never going be your friend. It's a bad wish." Her voice was calm and as flat as a tortilla. No emotion at all. "You shouldn't waste wishes like that."

Okay, pretty weird, right? But instead of freaking me out, it just made me angry. I snapped, "What do you know about anything? You don't know me."

I turned away to fumble with my combination lock.

"Twenty-two right, eleven left, seven right," she said, and walked away.

I called after her. "Hey, how'd you know my combination?"

"Psychic powers," she replied, turning to face me. And after a beat, "We've been locker neighbors since school started, not that you've noticed. You mumble your combination out loud every time you turn the dial."

I felt like an idiot, like a guy who couldn't tie his shoelaces without telling himself a story about the bunny that runs around the tree and down the hole.

"It's cute," she said, teeth sparkling with a mouth full of rubber bands and metal.

Cute? Seriously?

Didn't she realize I was dead?

DEAD BAT ON THE SIDE OF THE ROAD

After a month of school, I felt . . . nothing. Not angry, or sad, or lonely. Mostly I felt numb.

I had embraced my inner zombie.

The dead part of me.

The weird thing was, the more I watched kids at school, the more they looked like me. As if I were staring into a fun-house mirror that multiplied my image by the dozen. Zombies, zombies everywhere.

For example, Desmond Richardson was in a few

of my classes, average in every way. Dez watched the right television shows, rooted for the right teams, wore the standard sweatshirt and jeans and the popular sneakers. He had erased whatever might have been singular about his personality—whatever might have set him apart in any way. Now he fit in perfectly. On the surface, there was nothing different about Dez from everyone else in seventh grade. Most days Dez came into class dead tired, dragging his feet, shoulders slumped, lids barely lifted, eyes glassy.

And it wasn't just him.

When I looked around school, I realized that I was surrounded by semi-zombies, a crowd of conformists shuffling down the halls to science lab and social studies. They stayed up too late, rose too early, and looked like zonked-out cadavers wandering the halls in hopes of making honor roll—or at least surviving till the bell rang and they were released. And those were the kids who called me zombie, freak face, gimp, flyboy, loser. I got the irony of that, I really did.

After the last bell rang, I usually found Zander

waiting by the main doors. We hated the bus, its foul smells and many terrors, so most days we walked home together. Today he was leaning against the wall, his head tilted toward the pages of a slender book: *Hive Mind: The Secret Life of Honeybees*. All around him, the building was rapidly emptying, a liquid rush of students sloshing out the doors.

Deep into his reading, Zander could have been stranded on Mars for all he knew. He chewed on a Twizzler.

I tapped him on the shoulder and we walked.

Lately, in these last warm afternoons of early autumn, I'd been followed by a small but persistent swarm of flies. They must have been attracted to my smell. I'd taken to splashing on massive quanti ties of cologne to counter the stench of decay. It only made me reek of swamp. And still the flies loved me.

MaryAnne Lester, a girl in my English class, had even said to me, "I pray that some day you boys will learn that slathering yourselves in lime-scented anti-perspirant is not a substitute for a shower!"

She had a point.

I took it as a compliment, though. MaryAnne hadn't singled me out. I was just as malodorous as all the other boys. I had made the team!

Zander asked if I wanted to go to Leo's for a slice. I told him I sure did.

In case anybody's wondering, I could eat food; I just didn't digest it in a normal way. I would chew and swallow like everybody else, but my body didn't seem to process the nutrition efficiently. The food came and soon left, as if transported by a conveyor belt.

Sorry, maybe that's too much information.

Zander and I debated what makes a great slice. I claimed it was the sauce. Zander was sure it was the crust, which he liked thin and slightly burnt. Either way, we agreed that Leo's served the best pizza in town. It had a few small tables where we could sit, sip a cold drink, and chill.

I kept seeing my mother's face as we trudged through the streets. Whenever she got a new house to sell, she put up a sign in front of it. Free advertising. The sign was a buttery golden color with the words FOR SALE in fat red letters. Above it was a photo of my capable, confident mom, with the tag-line ANOTHER ROSIE LAZARUS LISTING.

I couldn't walk three blocks without seeing one of those stupid signs. There she was, watching over me, the Real Estate Queen. And lately that's where I saw her most, since she wasn't home much any-more. She said it was the demands of the job, but I wondered if having a zombie in the house drove her away. I mean, wouldn't you want to get out if your kid was a reanimated corpse, decomposing on the living room couch?

Boy, I would. And I'm me. I couldn't blame her if she hated me.

Zander narrowed his eyes, stopped in front of a house, and pointed toward a bush. "Wow, check that out."

We walked onto the lawn and stood near the base of an oak tree. It was a dead bat. Zander found a stick and gently poked it. He took a long look.

I said, "I've never seen a dead bat before."

It was entirely brown, except for the area around its nose, which was white. The body looked like a mouse's, but with the head of a tiny pig. Its ears were comically large, I guess for the radar thingy that helps bats fly at night. *Echolocation*, that's the word. Up close, its glossy wings looked like thin plastic, stretched from forelimbs to hind legs. All in all, an exotic creature that was perfectly adapted to a strange life.

Zander looked up at me, blinking. "This is so sad."

"It's a dead bat," I said. "What's sad about it?"

"It's like the honeybees," Zander said. "Remember Ms. Fjord talking about bats?"

I told Zander that perhaps I might not have been paying any attention whatsoever on the day of the bat story. Ms. Fjord, after all, told a lot of stories—it was hard to keep track. "Is this on the test?" we'd ask. And if it wasn't, we'd tune her out.

She didn't seem to care about tests as much as other teachers did, which many of her students found confusing. Tests were how we were measured, after all. As one kid asked, "If there's no test, what's the point?"

Zander was kneeling beside the dead bat. "This

isn't just about one dead bat, Adrian. There's a plague all across the eastern states," my friend, the walking, talking, weird-fact encyclopedia, told me. "More than seven million dead bats in the last five years."

"Okay, that's pretty bad."

"It's way worse than pretty bad," Zander countered. He reached into his back pocket and ripped off another Twizzler. He offered me one. Since there was something fundamentally gross about staring at a bat while chewing on a Twizzler, I declined. Zander explained, "Bats eat insects. And insects spread disease . . . to people. Bats in New York and some other states have been almost completely wiped out by white-nose syndrome."

He pointed with the stick at the bat's nose. It was strangely white.

"How do you know this stuff?" I asked. "What do you do all day?"

"You know I don't care about sports," Zander said. "That frees up a lot of time for reading."

"Yeah, but—"

"Think about all the basketball statistics you

know," Zander challenged me. "All that useless information cluttering your brain."

"So instead of knowing that Kobe Bryant won five championship rings . . ."

Zander nodded. "I know that brown bats are headed for the endangered species list."

"Do you think any of this stuff . . . explains me?"

Zander laughed. "Adrian, nothing explains you! All I know is nature is off balance. Climate change. Polar bears losing their habitat, dying out. Honeybees and bats disappearing. Zombies appearing."

I wondered, once again, if maybe I wasn't alone. "Do you think there's more than just me?"

Zander stood, puffing from the effort. "What? You figure you're the only one?"

I waved away a fly, shrugged my shoulders. "I don't know. But wouldn't we have heard if there were more?"

Zander sucked thoughtfully on his lower lip. "If I was a zombie? I'd keep it under my hat, you know. Who needs the abuse?"

Maybe he was onto something. Were other zombies out there? Not just one or two, but lots of us? Kids in other towns, closeted away out of sight? Zombies in basements, playing video games, afraid to come out? We'd hear about it, right? I wondered how many people knew about me. Not just rumors and gossip, but really knew the truth. If people heard the story that some random kid had turned into a zombie, would anyone even believe it?

Doubtful.

Maybe that's why Dr. Halpert worked so hard to keep things quiet. He said I'd been through enough, that I didn't need the distraction. No television interviews, no reporters. Which was fine with me because: Obviously!

Zander interrupted my reverie. "Come on, let's go get a slice. I'm getting one of those giant-size sodas—and I'm not sharing, so deal with it."

Leo's was your basic pizza joint. The neon sign outside read LEONARDO DI PIZZA! We called it Leo's for obvious reasons. The place was empty and had a nice, oven-warm feel to it. Cozy. There were two hairy guys behind the counter—Hasan, making the pies, his arms covered with flour, and a new guy I didn't recognize handling the orders and walk-in traffic. He had a thick black mustache and oven burns up and down his tattooed, muscular arms. He stared at me and his eyes darkened, as if a shadow had fallen over them. I pulled down my baseball cap and asked Zander to get me an Orange Crush. He screwed up his face, like *I'm not your waiter*, then it registered. No restaurant owner wanted to see my face walk into the place. I wasn't exactly an advertisement for fine dining. I grabbed a window seat on the far side of the room.

Zander returned with two slices and an enormous Coke, along with my orange drink. "Soon we're not going to need money. Everybody's going to have neck chips instead."

"What?"

"I read it online," Zander said. "It's a new deal set up by K & K Corp. You go to the bank, and the teller zaps a micro-nano-computer-chip thingy into your neck. Then when you buy something in stores, they scan it and the money is automatically deducted from your account."

"I don't have any money," I said.

"Well, that's a problem," Zander said. "Why aren't you eating?"

"I'm fine," I replied.

The door jingled. It was the tall girl from school. My locker neighbor, Gia Demeter. She glanced at us, unsurprised, and took a seat a few tables away. She didn't go to the counter to order. She sat down, opened a book—an actual, old-fashioned book— and started reading.

"That's the girl I told you about," I whispered to Zander.

"Yeah, I've seen her," Zander said. "I get a weird vibe."

Gia looked up as if she knew we were talking about her. Puzzled, wondering why.

"What are you looking at?" I called to her.

Gia ducked her head back into the book.

"Hello?" I said. "I asked you a question. Are you following us?"

She paused, glancing around, and said in a whisper, "For the record, I'd advise against the neck chips. That's how they'll keep track of you."

Zander shifted around in his chair to take a good look at this girl. "How did you know—?"

"You shouldn't use plastic straws, either," Gia said, gesturing to our table. "Or don't you care about the planet?"

"It's just a straw," I said.

"Scientists predict that by the year 2050, the ocean will have more plastic, pound for pound, than fish," Gia said.

Zander paused. "Wait, is that true?"

"More or less, best guess, it's the way things are going. Don't blame me, I'm only thirteen," Gia said.

"How do they estimate the weight of the fish?" Zander asked.

"Never mind the fish," I said, growing impatient. "Why are you even here?"

"I wanted to be here when it happens," she said.

Zander looked at me, shook his head, circled a finger near his ear in the universal sign for *crazy as a loon*.

But she'd gotten my attention. "When what happens?"

"You'll see soon enough," she said. "I thought maybe I could help."

Bang! Daryl Northrup slapped two hands against the front store window, not ten inches from my head, hard and loud. Daryl was on the outside looking in, surrounded by a group of pals. I stared back at them, wondering why they wouldn't just leave me alone. Daryl pointed at me, called back to his friends, "Hey, guys, look what I just found. It's the freak and his fat friend. And nobody around to protect them."

"Uh-oh," Zander said. He put down the slice.

I felt a rope twist in my stomach.

Gia turned down the corner of a page to mark the spot. She closed the book, slid it neatly to the far left corner of the table, loosened her neck from side to side like a boxer before entering the ring, and waited for the fecal matter to hit the fan.

FIGHT

"Yo, Adrian," Daryl called. "Come out and play."

"Freaky-deaky," sang a voice, and others chimed in, laughing.

Another yelled, "Spook!"

I didn't like that last one. Not at all. I wanted to charge out the door, fists flying, but I realized that's exactly what they wanted. I felt trapped.

Zander shrank in his chair, shoulders lowering, like he hoped to sink into the linoleum floor. I felt guilty that I'd involved Zander in my troubles.

"You chicken?" Daryl called. "You pus-faced, ugly piece of slime."

"Ignore it," Gia said. "Don't listen to them."

Daryl leaned against a parked car, crossed his arms. "No worries, no hurries. We'll wait."

There was no doubt in my mind why they were waiting and what they hoped to do. The names came, the insults in singsong voices: wuss, pukeface, drooler, zombie.

They didn't know the real me.

And to be honest, I wasn't so sure about the real me, either. Real or unreal, dead or alive, I decided to wait them out. To calm my jangled thoughts, I imagined a giant meteor falling from space and landing on top of them. The only thing left would be a smoking hole where their incinerated bodies used to be. "Poor Daryl, that must have hurt," I'd say, and take a lazy sip of my Orange Crush.

Daryl rolled into the store, sauntered up to the counter, bought a slice like a regular customer, super considerate. He pulled up a chair next to me.

"Duuuuude," he said.

"What is your problem?"

Daryl smirked, then wiped his greasy fingers on Zander's shirt. He helped himself to the soda on the table, burped. "My problem . . . is that you smell like death, you freak, and I'm going to kick your butt up and down this sidewalk."

"Don't," Gia warned.

Daryl spun around. "Who . . . in the hell . . . are you?"

Things happened quickly. I started to stand, and Daryl pushed me back into the chair. My head hit the window. Gia grabbed at Daryl, who shoved her away, and I launched a right hook to his chin.

A loud noise came from the counter behind us. The mustached pizza guy held a metal bat high in his hand. He pointed to the door. "Out!"

"But we didn't start it—" Zander began to argue.

"Out of my place now, or I'm calling the police," the man demanded.

We stepped outside, helplessly. Daryl stood a full head above me, with wide shoulders and blind hatred in his eyes. He turned away from me, head ducking down, then turned back and landed a sharp, compact punch to my face.

I didn't feel a thing, but I knew it wasn't going to improve my looks.

"That's it, I'm calling 911," Zander said, pulling out his cell.

With a swipe, Daryl knocked the phone to the ground. "Nobody's calling nobody," he said. "This is between me and the freak."

"Please," Zander reasoned.

Daryl punched him in the stomach. Zander doubled over, gasping for air.

I felt a fury rising up inside me, the way fierce winds gather to create a storm.

I heard myself scream:

"GET OUT OF HERE NOW OR I'LL FIRE-TRUCKING EAT YOUR BRAAAIIINS!"

Only I didn't say "fire-trucking." Because, like, who would? Is it even a word? No, I said a different f-word, one that I had heard before, plenty of times (I used to ride the school bus, after all). But I'd never said it out loud until that moment. I didn't mean to say it.

Well, no, that's not exactly right. I spewed it. I meant it the way a volcano means lava. I just didn't plan on saying it. Maybe it was the shock of that word, or the wild, crazed look in my eyes, but it totally worked. Everything stopped for a minute, as if the sidewalk tilted slightly. Everybody stood there, feeling the shift, wondering if anyone else felt it, too. It took a second for the boys to regain their balance. In that pause, no one moved, no one spoke. Daryl was the first to falter. He stepped back, as if blown by a stiff wind. I held my ground, shuddering, hands clenched in fists.

"Easy, freak," Daryl purred. "Don't get all bent. I'm only goofing around."

"Get out of here, you creeps." It was Gia's voice, strong and clear, coming from behind me. "Or you'll really be sorry."

Daryl stared at Gia as if seeing her for the first time. His friends turned their shoulders sideways, looked away, a wolf pack signaling surrender. "Sure, sure," Daryl said in a false show of cool. "We're good, we're gone."

"Apologize!" Zander bellowed. All eyes turned

to him in shock, the nowhere boy who'd been inconsequential until that moment. Zander seemed to stand taller. "Apologize now, like you mean it, or Adrian will make sure that bad, bad things happen to you."

"He'll chew your bones," Gia threatened in a soft voice. "He'll eat your heart."

"One bite and he'll zombify your butt," Zander stated.

A couple of the guys laughed nervously.

I stepped forward, dragging my one bad leg. "Try me," I said, voice scarcely above a whisper. "I haven't eaten in weeks."

And then, right there in front of Leonardo di Pizza, fueled by the strength of the undead, I feasted on their flesh.

NOT REALLY

Kidding.

ACTUALLY

Actually, they dispersed. The pack's threat fizzled away. Those guys did the internal calculations, the mathematics of risk and reward, and figured I wasn't worth the trouble. Because that's the way it is with all bullies. They play the odds, and they never risk a fair fight. Did they really think I could hurt them? With one vicious bite, turn them into flesh-crazed zombies? Or did they look into my wild eyes and see a dark, shadowy something that made them hesitate?

Nobody wants to fight the crazy guy.

I momentarily felt triumphant. I'd stood up to the creeps and trolls. Even better, I'd scared those guys out of their shoes.

The coast clear, Zander pounded on my back. "That! Was! Awesome!" he cried, smiling ear to ear, practically jumping out of his sneakers.

Gia didn't join in the celebration. She stood downcast, watching me. Under her gaze, my mood shifted.

"Why are they like that?" I asked her.

"You're different," she said. "And people hate you for it."

I didn't understand.

Gia stepped closer. "You are the scariest thing they can possibly imagine. You are not exactly like everybody else in school—and to them, that's an insult."

"Hey," Zander spoke up. "What makes you think you know so much?"

Gia stared at him, unblinking. "I've been different my whole life."

She turned to walk away.

"Hey, wait up," I said. "You said you came here to help me. How did you know—?"

"That something bad was about to happen?" Gia said, finishing my sentence. "I just knew. You're not the only one with a gift."

"A gift? You call this—"

"You're here, aren't you?"

"Yeah, in an undead kind of way," I countered. "But in there, you said you were here to help. I didn't see you lift a finger."

"I stood by you," she said. "Just like your friend here . . ."

"Zander," he said.

"Zander," she echoed, as if burning the name into memory. "That was all you needed this time, so that's all the help I gave."

She had the most incredible haunting green eyes. "What else could you have done?" I asked. "Are you a black belt in karate? A ninja warrior or something?"

Gia didn't say a word. Just bowed her head slightly, nodded politely in Zander's direction, took a few steps backward, turned, and left.

"Where you going?" I asked.

"Home," she said. "Getting late."

Zander and I watched her drift down the sidewalk, like a puff of smoke. "That Gia is—I mean, that girl—" Zander struggled and failed to find the words. He finally said, "She's kind of out there. Am I right?"

I didn't answer.

I was just glad to have one more person in my corner. Zombies can't be choosers.

HAMBURGERS
AND GAS MASKS

"Hello . . . ?"

Dane's uncertain voice called from the TV room.

"It's just me, Dane." I dropped my backpack with a thud.

Dane entered the mudroom, slipping on stocking feet. "I'm hungry."

"You're home alone? Where's Mom?"

Dane shrugged, blinking his small, round eyes. Poor guy.

I asked, "How'd you get home from school?"

"Mom picked me up, then she got a call and—"

"And left you here alone," I said.

"It's not her fault," Dane replied protectively. "She had to work."

I saw the worry lines under his eyes. Sometimes Dane looked like an old man in the body of a four-year-old. "Did something happen? Are you okay?"

Dane's face squinched up. He hurled himself at my legs and wrapped his short arms around me, and the floodgates opened up.

"Hey, hey, little man, what's this?" I said, rubbing his back. "Don't cry."

"You were supposed to come home right after school," he sputtered between sobs. "Mom said you'd be home in a jiffy."

I checked my cell. It was after five o'clock. No calls, no messages. "You should have called me. I didn't know. Nobody told me. Anyway, I'm home now."

"Good, because I'm starving." He broke into a

chubby-cheeked, fighting-back-the-sadness grin. My little brother, the human garden gnome, was undeniably cute. We went into the kitchen, where I poked around the shelves and cupboards, offering suggestions. "Cereal? Pretzels? I could nuke you some mac and cheese in the microwave."

"I wan' a burger," Dane said.

"Seriously? I don't have time to cook a whole dinner, Dane," I said. "I've got homework and—"

It was useless. Dane bit his lower lip and looked at me through eyes of sorrow. So I pulled out the frying pan, found a pound of hamburger meat in the fridge, and formed a patty with my hands. It was like making a meat snowball. "You like 'em thin or thick?" I asked.

"Thin, with cheese," Dane ordered. "Two slices. And ketchup."

"Yes, master," I said in a deep voice, hunching over and lurching toward his seat at the table.

Dane laughed.

"That's my impression of Igor, Dr. Frankenstein's hunchbacked assistant," I told him. Rubbing my hands together, I asked in a thick Transylvanian accent, "Anything else, massssterrr?"

"Soda," Dane said.

"Milk," I countered.

I leaned against the island countertop while Dane munched happily, idly watching the TV by the sink. One of Dane's favorite commercials came on, some company selling gas masks. A series of shots showed various models walking around while wearing the masks—shopping at the mall, standing in an elevator, moving down a crowded hallway, even at a cocktail party. Anytime there were lots of people around, a gorgeous body in a gas mask was among them. The commercial cut to a close-up of a blond actress. She yanked off her mask and smiled at us.

"EarthFirst Gas Masks," she announced. "Sleek and stylish and eighty percent more effective than ordinary surgical masks for protection against air pollution and other contagion!"

Her white teeth gleamed, her glossy red lips glistened, and something inside me stirred. Next, a handsome actor with flecks of gray in his hair stepped beside her. "That's right, Vanna. These masks will keep you safe from airborne diseases like dengue fever and superflu and"—he paused to shake his head, winking mischievously—"who knows what other germs are floating around out there nowadays! I know I'm not taking chances!"

Vanna laughed. *Ho-ho-ho.*

I turned off the TV.

"Hey!" Dane protested.

"You don't need to watch that stuff," I said. "It'll fry your brains."

"I want one for Christmas," Dane said.

"Christmas? Already? Let's get past Halloween first. Then you can write to Santa," I said. "I think there's a new line of masks coming out just for kids. I read there's even going to be a Darth Vader mask."

Dane sat swinging his feet in the air, munching silently, probably imagining himself in a Darth Vader gas mask. He stopped chewing and looked at me with a funny expression. "Shouldn't you cook it first?" he asked. He pointed at the package of raw hamburger meat.

I discovered that I had a hunk of raw meat in my hand . . . and in my mouth. I immediately spit it into the sink—disgusting!—and rinsed my mouth with water. "What the heck!" I said, bringing a hand to my suddenly churning stomach. I saw that almost all the raw meat from the package was gone. "Why didn't you tell me sooner? I didn't know I was eating it."

Dane bit into his burger. A trickle of grease rolled down his chin, shimmering in the light. "I didn't know people could eat hamburger meat without cooking it."

"Don't tell Mom, okay? I don't want her to get more freaked out than she already is."

Dane nodded.

"Remember to put the dishes in the sink when you're done," I reminded him. "I'm going up to my room."

I trudged up the stairs, head spinning. What was happening to me?

That night an explosive storm shook the trees. Jagged lightning bolts slashed the sky like silvery swords swung by Greek gods. The rain was hard and relentless, pelting the windows like thrown gravel. I wondered if it was all connected some-how—a giant tapestry of connect-the-dots. I was a reanimated corpse, alone in the world, but I also sensed that maybe I was part of something larger.

The bats and the bees and the fish in the seas.

And me?

I slipped downstairs to finish off the rest of the hamburger meat.

It was delicious.

What was going on with my taste buds?

When I returned to my room, Dane was sitting on my bed, arms curled tight around his knees. The wind roared outside, and a tree limb fell nearby.

"What's up, Dane? Can't sleep?"

Dane's sweet face was troubled. He looked at me and trembled, just a scared kid in action-hero paja-mas, not even two thousand days old. He said in an urgent whisper, as if delivering a forbidden secret, "The world is falling apart."

"There, there," I said lamely, sitting down next to him. "Now, now." I rubbed his back, touched his hair, tried to reassure him.

"I'm scared," he said.

"I know. I'm glad you came to find me," I said. "To tell you the truth, I was scared, too. Superstorms are like that. When we're together it's not so bad, right?"

Dane's eyes flickered. He nodded. "If you'll let me stay, we can be brave together."

I pulled out a sleeping bag from the hall closet. "You get the floor. Just don't snore." I threw a pillow at his head.

Dane laughed. Ever squirmy, he kicked and wriggled and rolled around in the bag, as relaxed as a cat in a burlap sack. He eventually settled down. I lay on my bed, blinking at the blank space above my head. "Hey, Dane," I whispered. "You still awake?"

"Mmmm," he answered dreamily.

"You don't care that I'm a zombie, do you?"

Dane was quiet for a long moment, and I wondered if he'd finally fallen asleep. Then he said in a soft voice, "Not really. Some people say things, but I don't care. I guess everybody's different, and nobody's perfect. I just want you to be happy again."

Smart kid, that little brother of mine. And I'll

say this: If I was a little bit squishier, if I had a drop more moistness in my dusty innards, I might have squeezed out a tear or two. I felt a shadowy fist, clenching and unclenching, where my heart used to beat. "Come up here," I said, sliding over to make room. "There's plenty of space for both of us."

TALAL MIRWANI,
PRIVATE EYE

Word had gotten around school about my encounter with Daryl, a brawling bully who, let's face it, was probably even less popular than me. I'm not saying I was suddenly the tightest guy shuffling down the halls. It was just that every once in a while somebody might say, "Oh, that's so great you were reanimated," and compliment me on how my limp wasn't so bad. I got friendly nods from strangers and fist bumps out of the blue, as if I'd just pitched a no-hitter.

It was nice to catch a break. Even so, I could tell that most kids were still mildly uneasy. I guess I couldn't blame them. Half of my nose actually fell off during science class on Tuesday—my nose!— and I had to slap it back on with glue from the art room. Talk about embarrassing. I started wearing hoodies pulled down low over my face like an unholy monk. I guess I was just an oddity on the school grounds, like a piece of furniture that didn't look right in any room. Nobody *actively* bothered me anymore.

I even stopped having to worry about Daryl. I'd see him in P.E., of course, but he steered away from me, not even bothering to glance in my direction. It was as if I'd scared away a bear at a campsite by banging on pots and pans. It worked for now, but I wondered if that bear might come back someday.

In the cafeteria on Wednesday, Zander and I discussed the desperate state of his fish tank. Actually, he talked—and talked, and talked—while I listened.

"What a disaster," he moaned. "My temperature regulator broke last night, but I didn't realize it until the morning—twenty minutes before I was supposed to leave for school. With tropical fish, that's not a major deal. But I've got a saltwater tank, so even minor fluctuations of temperature can amount to an environmental catastrophe.

"So I'm, like, stressing, thinking I'm going to lose the whole tank if I don't fix this right now, and meanwhile my mother is screaming from downstairs: 'Zander! Come down here and eat your breakfast!'

"So I screamed back at her, 'I'm not going to school, Ma!' "

"I bet she didn't like that," I said, just to squeeze a few words into the conversation.

"She was like, 'Oh yes you are, mister,' and I was like, 'Nuh-uh, these fish depend on me, Ma!' "

"So what did you do?"

"I was stressed exponentially, okay, to the tenth power, you understand that, right? I'm sweating buckets. But I took a deep breath and explained to my mother that I was like God to these fish. I'd created their entire world. I'd placed every plant and rock and piece of coral in that aquarium. I was the one who'd installed the purification system. If I couldn't get the temp and pH level fixed right away, I'd return home from school to an environmental disaster like one of those oil spills off the coast. My clown fish already looked green around the gills."

A slight kid walked up, wearing a fedora and a long brown raincoat. He had black hair and light brown skin. The boy placed a hand on the back of an empty chair and asked, "You gents mind?"

"It's all yours, no one's sitting there," I said, expecting him to drag the chair to another table. But to my surprise, he sat down with us.

Zander stopped talking and paused to stare at our uninvited guest. The look on Zander's face was basically: *What the what?*

"The name's Talal"—he pronounced it slowly, tah-LAHL, so we got it right—"but you can call me Tal. That's easier for most people," he said in a soothing voice. Talal rested an elbow on the back of the chair. He folded an ankle across a knee. "And you are the zombie guy," he added, turning to address me.

"That's me," I said. "The zombie guy."

"Why are you here?" Zander asked. "We're not bothering anybody."

"I'm a detective," Talal replied. "You could say that I'm working on a case."

"Uh-huh," I said.

"I prefer the term *gumshoe*," Talal continued, "except nobody knows what it means anymore. So, sure, I'm a private eye."

I decided to play along. "How can we help you, gumshoe?"

"Call me Tal. It's simpler."

"Okay, detective," I replied.

Zander glanced in my direction. He clearly didn't trust this new kid at our table. But as far as I could tell, Talal seemed harmless. Besides, I was curious.

Talal lifted the fedora off his head and placed it, ever so gently, on the table. He clawed his hand through his hair, as if scratching the back of an appreciative Labrador retriever.

"What makes you a detective?" Zander asked.

"What do you mean?" Talal asked.

Zander looked annoyed. His voice rose a notch in volume. "I mean, big deal, you say you're a detective. Anybody could say that. Saying so doesn't make it true."

Talal stared long and patiently. He slow-blinked once, twice, with all the urgency of a three-toed sloth. Then he fished in the depths of his trench coat pocket and produced a business card. He ran his thumb across the edge of it and, flicking two fingers, sent it spinning across the table and into my lap.

TALAL MIRWANI

Detective

NO CASE TOO LARGE OR SMALL

Talal turned to Zander. "Believe whatever you like. I'm what the card says I am."

Zander smiled. "And I'm a horned toad. There, I said it. Does that make it true?"

Talal was amused. "No, big guy, the saying doesn't

make it so. It's the believing that matters. You don't really think you're a toad, do you?"

Zander didn't answer.

"It's the believing in things that counts," Talal repeated for emphasis, "as long as you're asking."

"Like in Santa Claus?" Zander teased.

"Like in anything," Talal replied. "The tooth fairy, dinosaurs, zombies, kindness, whatever floats your boat." Talal returned the hat to the top of his head and deftly zipped a pointed index finger across the front brim. "I didn't come here to philosophize. You have my card."

"We don't need it," Zander said.

"Maybe not you, but I think *he* might," Talal said, jerking a thumb in my direction. "And I bet he knows it, too."

"I'm not going to hire a detective," I protested.

"It's already been handled," Talal replied. "Your friend paid for my services."

"My friend?" I couldn't think of anybody.

"A tall and angular girl," he intoned, "the angel looking over your shoulder. Cash in advance. Consider yourself lucky."

"Gia?"

Talal shrugged as if it didn't matter. "She said trouble's coming your way, and figured I might be able to steer you clear."

I struggled to process the information. My un-life was getting weirder by the minute. It felt like Gia had some sort of plan for me, but I had no idea what it was. Still, there was something oddly reassuring about Talal. He was a character, for certain, but I guess I heard Dane's voice in my ear: *Everybody's different, and nobody's perfect.*

Who was I to say that Talal wasn't good enough to sit at our table? There was plenty of room.

Zander, on the other hand, acted protective. "How are you going to help Adrian? All I see is a kid in a trench coat who talks tough, like you just stepped out of some old black-and-white movie. What do you know?"

Talal leaned back in his chair, calmly tented his fingers together. "What do I know? I'll tell you what I know . . ."

He spoke the next part in rapid pitter-pat style: "I know you had a rough time this morning. You barely had a minute to wolf down a bowl of Rice Krispies. You missed the bus, but that's no problem, because Mommy drives you anyway."

"Hold on," Zander said. "How did you know—?"

Talal explained. "There's a trace of shampoo in your right ear, your socks don't match, and there's a dried Rice Krispie kernel stuck to your shirt. Judging by the mud splatter on the cuffs of your jeans, I'd bet ten balloons you tried to jump the puddle by the curb at the student drop-off. You didn't quite make it. Don't feel too bad, champ—it's probably because of the extra twenty pounds of books you lug around in your backpack, because you are exactly the kind of kid who carries his books everywhere. I'd bet another ten balloons you make the honor roll every semester. You're smart and you work hard. That's a good thing, congratulations." Talal flicked a finger. "I can also see the pink edge of a late pass poking out of your shirt pocket. What else do I know? You're a little sloppy, but it doesn't take a detective to figure that out. More importantly, you are not the kind of guy who spends time in front of a mirror. Either you don't care how you look, or you care too much. So much that maybe it hurts. Hard for me to say, we've only just met, but I know this: Everybody cares, we just hide it in different ways."

Zander didn't need to hear any more. He squirmed in uncomfortable silence, like a living butterfly pinned to a wall. Talal turned out to be a pretty sharp detective after all.

DRONE ABOVE

Talal proved useful the very next day.

I never liked the trapped, shut-in feeling of a hundred sardines in a smelly tin, so I preferred walking home from school to taking the bus. Today Gia joined Zander and me, and Talal tagged along, too. We were an unusual group of misfits, but it felt okay. We didn't belong anywhere except with each other.

"Look at these green lawns," Gia sneered. She had recently dyed her hair a brilliant shade of purple. "It's such a waste."

"What do you mean? The lawns look fine to me," I said.

"Don't you know that it's against the law to water your lawn in some states?"

Zander shrugged, "Out west, yeah. Arizona, New Mexico, Nevada. Those places have a drought, water is scarce, but we're okay."

"For now," Gia said. "But in the future—

"Oh, don't start about the future," Zander scoffed. "You act as if you know what's going to happen, like you can see into the future, but you don't know. Nobody does."

It looked as if Gia was about speak—her mouth opened, a flame reached her eyes—but she appeared to decide against it. She simply muttered, "Don't be an ostrich, Zander. Head buried in the sand."

"I read, I know plenty," Zander rebuffed.

Talal didn't engage in the debate. He walked along without talking, dreamily gazing up into the autumn leaves.

Gia said, "These people run their sprinklers practically every day. They don't care if there's a water shortage. And why do they do it? For a bunch of grass we can't even eat. Lawns are so stupid."

"Goats like lawns," Talal commented. "The pale green shoots are tender to eat."

"People like lawns, too," I said. "My mom's in real estate. She says a good lawn adds value to a house. Curb appeal or something like that. It doesn't mean that—"

"Shhh." Talal held up his hand.

We stopped while Talal scanned the trees. "What is it?" Zander asked.

"Adrian," Talal said in a calm, measured voice, "do me a favor. Keep walking straight ahead. Zander and Gia, stay here with me."

"What? I don't—"

"Please, just do it."

The tone of Talal's voice told me he wasn't fooling around. So I did what he asked. As I walked, I glanced back at the others. Talal pointed up to the trees above my head and spoke quietly to Gia. After I'd walked about a hundred feet, Talal signaled for me to return.

Before I could ask questions, Talal explained,

"I'm conducting an experiment." He gestured for Gia and Zander to walk ahead, then split apart in different directions. As they walked, Talal squinted and searched the sky. "Interesting," he murmured. Talal cast his eyes over the ground and settled on a stone that was about the size of a golf ball. He picked it up and thoughtfully weighed its heft in his hand. "Now, Adrian, you go the other way," he said, pointing in the opposite direction.

I looked at him. "Seriously? What's the big mystery, Talal?"

"Go," he said, scarcely speaking the word out loud.

So go I did, walking up the road from where we came. I felt like an idiot. I turned in time to see Talal rear back to fire a rock into the branches twenty feet above my head. *Thwack*. A small brown bird fell at my feet, hitting the street with a tragic *thunk*.

"Why did you do that, Tal?" I screamed. "You can't go around stoning birds."

Talal raced forward. He bent down to examine the fallen creature.

"Nice shot," Zander said. "Is it what you thought it was?"

"Yes," Talal replied, tilting back the front of his hat with a thumb. "It's a drone."

"A drone?" I repeated.

"A drone," he said, now holding the mechanical object in his hands. It was about the size and general shape of a sparrow. Talal mused, "Could be a government model, or maybe Corporate. It's hard to tell the difference anymore. I'll have to take it apart in my workshop to know for sure."

I still didn't understand. "What's a drone doing here?"

Talal glanced at the others. "Don't you get it? You're being followed."

"Followed?"

"It's a spy drone," Talal said. "That's the easy part. The big question is, who is spying on Adrian Lazarus?"

"And why?" Zander added.

"Can you find out?" I asked.

Talal gently nestled the drone in his roomy coat

pocket, as if he were cradling a delicate bird. "I know a few people I can trust," he said. "Computer geeks, hackers. I'll take this problem to them. Good thing I tagged along with you guys today. Who knows how long that thing's been following you."

MORNING ANNOUNCEMENTS

On top of everything else, our principal was losing his mind. Maybe it was the job, I don't know. There were days when our school felt like a madhouse—and the students weren't the loony ones. Take today's morning announcement for example, which began as usual with an ear-piercing buzz:

Kkccchh. "Is this on?" *Kkccchh. Tap-tap, TAP-TAP.* "Miss Shen? Is this thing"—*whirr*—"hey-ho, ouch!—What the . . . ? Good mooooorningggg, Nixon Middle School! This is your principal, Mr. Rouster!"

From my seat in a back corner of my homeroom class, I watched as everyone turned to the loudspeaker in listless silence.

The substitute teacher, Mrs. Perez, never looked up from her smartphone. Principal Rouster crowed. "All righty, then! I've got some good news, some bad news, and some really bad news. First, the good news! Our school recently received a large federal grant involving enormous sums of taxpayers' money. I'm pleased to announce that there will be construction going on throughout the school. You may be inconvenienced by the occasional disruption."

On cue, a series of loud noises—banging, chiseling, and the vibrating cacophony of a jackhammer—erupted out in the hallway. Next came a calamitous crash, a thud, and a muffled "Oops."

Principal Rouster chattered on in a nasal voice, unruffled. "The bad news is that the construction will cause changes to our normal schedule. Until further notice, the cafeteria will be moved to the gymnasium. But P.E. will go on as scheduled. Just don't confuse the meatballs with the dodgeballs! Heh-heh. The Choir Club will share a room with the Chess Club; they will both meet in the science lab. On Tuesday we'll follow the Wednesday schedule, except for band members, who will adhere to their Thursday schedules—but only on Mondays. Lastly, the literacy center will be closed because of the asbestos problem recently brought to our attention by Janitor McConnell's alarming rash. Get better soon, Mike!"

The girl next to me, Desiree Reynolds, muttered, "I wonder what the really bad news is."

Principal Rouster continued. "The really bad news is that all bathroom privileges have been temporarily suspended. This should last only a few hours. In case of emergency, a temporary porta-potty has been set up in the main hallway. I don't have to tell you that with seven hundred students in the school, we'll require a high level of cooperation and an almost Zen-like self-control of your bodily fluids. Please avoid all liquids, and I strongly suggest that you tread lightly on today's lunch special, the New Orleans gumbo. That stuff runs right through you.

"Thank you and happy learning!"

TALAL CLUES ME IN

I was still asleep when Dane knocked on my bed-room door.

Key word: *was.*

Past tense.

"Go away," I grumbled.

"Your friend is here," Dane called through the door.

I looked at my clock. It was 8:15 on a Saturday morning. I sat up, holding my head in my hands. It felt heavy, like a large pumpkin. "Who is it?"

Dane poked his nose into the room. "I don't know. I never saw him before. He's wearing a raincoat. And, um, he's carrying two umbrellas."

Umbrellas? The sun's hazy glare streamed through my window. The sky was crisp blue, like an ironed shirt. For a moment, my mind still sputtering, I thought it could have been Zander. Then I remembered the coat. "His name is Talal," I told Dane. "Tell him I'll be right down."

"In your boxers?" Dane asked.

"Just go," I said.

When I arrived downstairs, I found Dane sprawled on the floor, working on an endangered-species puzzle. Pieces were scattered everywhere. I asked, "Where is he?"

Dane pointed to the side door.

"You didn't invite him in?"

"He wanted to wait outside," Dane replied.

I went to the sink to gulp down a large glass of water. Still working on hydration, you know. Out the kitchen window I spied Talal standing near our big, sad rhododendron, its leaves turned yellow and brown. Although it was a picture-perfect morning, Talal held a large black umbrella over his head. "I won't be long," I told Dane.

"Can I come?" he asked.

"Sorry, bud. Next time."

Outside, I squinted in the sunlight. I said, "You woke me up, Tal. Come on inside while I make a shake."

"I'd rather not do that," Talal said. "The walls have ears and eyes. Here." He opened an umbrella and handed it to me. "Hold this."

"Dude?"

"I'm serious," Talal said.

I studied his face. He wasn't joking.

"Let's walk and talk," he said. "It's about that drone. Leave your phone."

"My phone? I need it," I said.

Talal shook his head. "No phone."

"Okay, okay." I placed my cell on the patio table.

Talal walked toward the back gate. I caught up with him. We were an absurd sight, carrying open umbrellas on a sunny day.

"Do you know they can activate all the cameras inside our computers?" Talal asked. "You have a smart kitchen, right? Everything's run by computers. We don't have to remember to turn off the lights anymore. Cars drive themselves. Our machines automatically order kitty litter when we run low. Think about your phone. That spectacular piece of technology can record every word you say. It can locate exactly where you are. It knows what you ate for dinner and how many hours you sleep. Don't you understand? They see what you see."

"Whoa, ease up," I said. "Who are *they*?"

We walked along the street, close to the curb, not on the sidewalk. The roads were quiet. We had the sleepy town to ourselves.

Talal stopped. He pulled out a tiny computer chip sealed in a plastic bag. "I took that drone apart piece by piece," he said. "I talked to some people, geeks I trust who specialize in this kind of thing. We know who is spying on you."

I didn't know what to say. It was all kind of unreal.

"There's a tiny logo printed on this chip, invisible to the human eye," Talal said. "But when put under a microscope and magnified by the order of ten thousand, it's as clear as day."

He pulled a folded paper from his pocket. It was a printout of an enlarged image: the K & K logo.

"So?" I said.

"So?" Talal echoed. "This proves that the Bork brothers are interested in you. They own the richest, most powerful corporation on the planet. They practically run the country. Those guys live in a compound only forty-five miles away, up beyond a crest in the Catskills."

"Oh, right," I said, remembering. "I think I heard about them, maybe."

"They don't like the spotlight," Talal explained. "They operate in the shadows. But they are very powerful—real financial wizards, and ridiculously rich. They are the ones who sent the drone." He glanced around, eyes scanning restlessly. "They are probably trying to listen to this conversation right now."

"That's why you brought the umbrellas," I said.

"Lip-readers," Talal said. "Their staff could video-tape us without sound, then figure it out later. These guys will do anything to get the information they want."

"What information?" I protested. "I mean, even if what you say is true—that these Bork brothers are following me for some reason—I don't know anything! I'm just a kid. An average, run-of-the-mill—"

"Zombie," Talal interrupted. "Nothing average about you."

I felt like he'd punched me in the gut.

"Sorry, but that's the deal," Talal said. "As far as I know, you might be the only person who has died and yet still lives. That makes you different. And maybe it makes you interesting."

We turned down one block, then another. "Can we sit?" I suggested. "My ankle."

"Sure," Talal said. He led us to a stone bench in the back of a nearby churchyard. He pulled a sheaf of papers out of his deep coat pocket. "I put this packet together last night. Sorry it's sloppy. I didn't have much time."

The pages were neatly folded and stapled along the left edge. There was nothing haphazard about the way Talal worked. The top page featured a black-and-white photograph of infant twins, swaddled under blankets, in a hospital setting. The twins are turned toward each other as if whispering a secret.

Beneath the photo, a caption read, THE ONLY CHILDHOOD PHOTOGRAPH OF WALL STREET WIZARDS KALVIN AND KRISTOFF BORK.

I flipped the page.

The next photo was of the twins again. But this time they were aged men, heads close together, unsmiling, staring directly at the camera. Once again, a large blanket covered their bodies from their necks down. At their knees, four identical legs poked out, wearing matching black socks and leather shoes.

"They look . . ."

Talal turned to me. "They look . . . what?"

"I don't know. Just weird, I guess."

Talal nodded, not saying anything.

I flipped through the rest of the pages. They were filled with numbers, charts, and newspaper clippings.

"What do we do now?" I asked.

"Nothing," Talal said. "At least nothing right now. Let me see what I can dig up on these guys. In the meantime, get used to sometimes going without a cell phone. Let's not make it any easier for their people to spy on you."

We headed back toward my house. I had to check on Dane—he'd be worried. Talal stopped two blocks from my house. "We'll part here," he said. "I have a family thing."

"Sure," I said. "And, um . . . thanks, Tal."

Maybe he saw something in my face. He said, "Hey, Adrian. It'll be okay."

"Sure, sure," I repeated. And after a pause, I said, "You know, sometimes I have this crazy thought, but I've never told anyone."

Talal just watched me, unmoving, waiting.

I gestured to the trees and houses. "I sometimes wonder if all this is just a giant sim game run by a computer program for the amusement of super-beings. Do you ever think that?"

Talal actually laughed. "All the time," he replied with a grin.

I limped home, my stomach oddly rumbling. Looking up, I noticed a wake of redheaded turkey vultures, at least twenty of them circling in a vortex high above me, holding steady without flapping their wings. I'd never seen that many at once before. They spiraled hypnotically, round and round, riding pockets of warm air. Maybe they saw me with their keen eyes. Perhaps they were as puzzled by it all as I was.

I didn't have an answer for them.

"Sorry, birds," I murmured. "I haven't got a clue."

Dane was taking a bath when I got home. My mother was on the computer. I clicked on the television. A commercial came on. I'd probably seen it a hundred times before, but this time I noticed the names at the end of it.

The commercial flashed a series of short film clips, each more beautiful than the next. A fishing boat leaves a harbor, a man in a business suit gets into a cab, a rugged farmer drives a big-wheeled tractor, a cowboy saddles up, a car and a moving van pull into the driveway of a huge home, a teary-eyed grandmother watches a wedding scene in church, various citizens hoist American flags up flagpoles, rows of smiling children look up in wonder, a proud eagle soars across the sky. Final image: a logo on the side of a huge glass-and-steel building for K & K Corp.

While all those images floated past, a man's voice spoke in soothing tones. The words scrolled across the screen in block letters as he spoke:

BE AT PEACE.

THERE IS NOTHING TO WORRY ABOUT.

ALL IS GOOD, ALL IS WELL.

THE BIRDS ARE SINGING.

IT IS MORNING IN AMERICA.

BE HAPPY. RELAX. SMILE.

WE ONLY CARE ABOUT YOUR HAPPINESS.

In smaller print, it read: THIS HAS BEEN A PAID ADVERTISEMENT BY K & K CORP.

"That's some frown, Adrian," my mother said.

She had joined me in the kitchen and was poking around in the refrigerator. "What's bothering you?"

"Huh? What?" I replied. "Nothing, I'm fine. I was watching that commercial and—"

"Don't you love it?" my mother said while slicing into a giant, perfectly pink, wonderfully round, genetically engineered grapefruit. "I see that commercial every day, and every day it makes me smile."

I made an effort to smile right along with her.

"Be happy. Relax. Smile," my mother repeated. "Those are words to live by!"

I didn't answer. Instead, I wondered why K & K Corporation was spending millions of dollars on commercials to brainwash all of us.

They didn't want us to worry.

Because of course they didn't.

Everything was fine.

Be happy. Relax. Smile.

I went up to my room and sprawled across the bed. I felt a strong urge to find Gia. She had an eerie knack for knowing what was about to happen. It was time we had a talk.

My cell dinged. It was a message from Gia:

7:30 tonight. Flattop Hill. Go to the bench that faces the tracks. We need to talk.

Once again, she was two moves ahead of me.

UNDER A
HOLOGRAM SKY

Flattop Hill was a famous park in our town. Flat on top—thus the name—it overlooked the river. There was a grass meadow about the size of a soccer field, where people picnicked, sunbathed, played ball, and tossed Frisbees to bounding dogs. I guess they did other stuff, too. But you get the point. People recreated on Flattop Hill like there was no tomorrow.

Getting to it wouldn't be easy. It would be the first time I attempted to ride a bicycle since the accident. Because my old bike was DOA (like me, I guess), I borrowed Zander's; he barely used it. Exercise and healthy living were totally not Zander's cup of tea. Come to think of it, a cup of tea was not Zander's cup of tea. He preferred soda and didn't worry about the sugar. What can I say? Zander was a nearly round ball of inconsistencies. He worried about the future of the bees but not about the fate of his own incisors. Best friend ever.

If I was apprehensive about getting on a bike again, my fears soon faded away. After a block or two, I remembered how much I loved the feeling of rolling past houses with the wind in my face. I almost felt free.

But the ride was long and difficult, since I wasn't exactly in tip-top shape. I ditched Zander's bike at the bottom of the hill and climbed a steep path to the top. When I arrived, huffing and puffing like the Big Bad Wolf, I glimpsed Gia seated on a bench. Her back was to me. It was dusk, and a fading sun dropped into the river. Gia turned and did not appear surprised to see me approaching, as if she knew the exact moment I would arrive.

"Hurry up, Adrian," she called.

"What do you expect me to do? Break into a jog?"

"I want you to stop dragging that leg." She smiled. "And come sit down next to me. Stop feeling sorry for yourself."

"You think my problem is I've got a bad attitude?" I felt sticky and irritable. "How about the fact that my ankle sucks and, oh yeah, I almost forgot: I died this August."

Gia tucked a strand of hair behind her ear. "I'm trying to help you, but I can't if you won't get over yourself. So, fine, you died. But now here you are. With me. Here and now. So what's the big deal?"

"My nose fell off last week!" I protested. "I went to scratch my face and, plop, it landed on page fifty-seven of my science textbook."

"Like you're the only middle schooler with skin problems," Gia scoffed. "Get an appointment with a dermatologist. *Oh, I'm a zombie. Boo-hoo.* Guess what? I had my braces tightened last week. You don't hear me complaining."

"Seriously?"

Her mouth shaped into a grin. And then she started laughing, softly at first, then harder. I guess it was infectious. I laughed, too.

"Your nose actually fell off in the middle of class?" Gia asked.

"Super embarrassing," I confessed.

We both laughed. Life was comical when you looked at it a certain way.

"It would have been funnier if you'd sneezed and your nose shot across the room like a spitball, boom, splat," Gia joked.

"Yeah, thanks," I said. "I'll work on that next time."

Gia looked directly at me. There was something new in her eyes, a kindness. "You know, Adrian Lazarus," she said, "it looks fine now. I'd never know that your nose fell off if you hadn't told me."

"Well, I don't know about that," I said. "It seems like you know a lot of things. But thanks for saying so."

Gia slid over to make room on the bench. I sat down. The sunset looked good through the radiation clouds. The reds just a little redder. The pinks a little pinker. The whole sky was like the planet itself, I mused: just a big, beautiful bruise. Like somebody had socked it in the eye.

"My mother says there used to be more stars in the sky," Gia said, gazing up. "Millions, billions, like salt spilled across a black countertop."

"Stars don't usually get up and go," I said. "It's the same number as always."

Gia shook her head. "We changed the sky, Adrian, just like we changed the planet. You need to understand that. We're living in the Anthropocene era now."

"The what?" I asked

"Oh, look!" Gia exclaimed. "The hologram advertisements are about to begin!"

The night sky flared bright pink, then blue. Then the lasers began, flashing a series of astonishing holographic lights across the night's dark canvas, proudly brought to us by our sponsors at FoodTech, K & K, EduCorp, et cetera, et cetera, and on and on.

"Let us go then, you and I," Gia murmured to herself, "to watch the advertisements in the sky!"

"Excuse me?"

"Not too long ago, billboards used to line the highways," Gia said. "People thought the billboards were ugly, but they let it happen anyway. Money talks, right? They took this beautiful planet—a landscape of mountains, fields, and rivers—and put up huge, hideous billboards advertising junk food and cars. In most places, anyway. A few states passed laws against it. Some communities, a select few, refused to sell every last inch of beauty on the planet. But look at that sky, Adrian. Corporate has put powerful spotlights out by the mall, and they advertise in the sky for free."

I idly watched a few commercials for things I didn't need. A lively commercial came on for Pretty Pillz: HAVE YOU TAKEN YOUR PRETTY PILL TODAY? Soon, it claimed, everyone would be beautiful—it was as easy as swallowing a pill. Scenes floated past of gorgeous people romping around, flashing perfect smiles. Then a long line of type scrolled across the sky: WARNING: SIDE EFFECTS OF PRETTY PILLZ

MAY INCLUDE DROWSINESS, IRRITABILITY, STOM-
ACH PAIN, DIARRHEA, NAUSEA, MEMORY LAPSES,
BACK PAIN, AN INABILITY TO DIFFERENTIATE BE-
TWEEN THE COLORS GREEN AND BLUE, LOSS OF
HEARING, RINGING IN THE EARS, IRREGULAR HEART-
BEAT, SUDDEN VISION LOSS, NIGHT SWEATS, SHORT-
NESS OF BREATH, SUICIDAL URGES, AND DEATH.
OTHERWISE, IT'S ALL GOOD!

"What a world," I said.

"Don't blame our generation," Gia said. "We didn't make it."

"No, we just inherited it." I shifted in my seat to look Gia in the eye. "So why did you ask me here?"

GIA'S STORY

"I'm like you," Gia said.

Her eyes did not leave mine.

"Like me . . . how?"

"We're the same because we're both different,"
Gia said.

"Oh." I didn't understand.

"Something happened to me, Adrian. The way
something happened to you."

"Just say it, Gia. What happened to you?"

"You know I'm not from around here," Gia said.
"My mother and I used to live in Virginia."

"No father?" I asked.

Gia shook her head sharply. No father.

"I loved it there. We had a forest preserve near my house. It had a maze of little wooded pathways. I used to walk in that forest all the time, under the cool shade of trees. I learned all their names: cedar and pine, hickory and cottonwood.

"The problem is that I'm allergic to bees. It's not that uncommon. I'm supposed to carry an EpiPen, but after they became so obscenely expensive, we couldn't afford one. I usually carried around a sandwich bag with some Benadryl pills, but not always. I figured that one sting wouldn't be that dangerous. Pretty dumb, I guess.

"One morning I went out for a walk. I never got too far that day. I'm still not sure exactly what happened. I probably stepped on an old stump or something and accidentally disturbed a hive. In an instant, I was surrounded by an angry swarm of bees."

"Oh my God," I said.

"It was crazy, Adrian. I felt a sting on my arm, then another on my neck. I swatted and ran. But the bees were everywhere, buzzing and stinging. When I tried to take in air, I only heard a whistling sound. I was wheezing, my chest felt tight. It was so scary, I couldn't—"

Gia didn't finish the sentence. Her gaze was far away, remembering the nightmare of that day.

"I fell to the ground, covered with bees," Gia said. "And I guess I passed out."

"Did someone find you?"

Gia shook her head. "When I opened my eyes, I was alone. I didn't know how many hours had passed. It was near dark. The bees were gone. The forest was still. I felt—I don't know how to describe it—do you know those Greek myths where people turn into swans? Or that guy who turns into a flower?"

"Narcissus," I said.

"Yes, exactly," Gia said. "Shape-shifters. The old world was filled with those fantastical stories. Tales of men who transform into pigs. Girls who become spiders. A hunter who is turned into a stag, only to be devoured by his own dogs."

"What happened to you?" I asked.

Gia shrugged, pushed the hair from her face. "I

woke up. I was alive, and I wasn't supposed to be alive," she said. "I felt, I don't know, strong. Powerful, even. There was no one around. Perfect stillness. That's when I saw her, the queen bee. She sat on my chest, and I swear, Adrian, we regarded each other in perfect silence, like equals. She saw the real me, staring back at her. And she spoke."

"The queen? Spoke?"

"I know how it sounds," Gia said. "But I need you to listen. Somehow, some way, the queen communicated with me. Three words. And then she was gone."

I waited. "Well, don't leave me hanging. What did she say?"

"She said, '*It all connects.*'"

Pure craziness, right? There was no reason to believe Gia's story, but of course I believed every word. Maybe I was the only person who could. As Gia said, we were the same because we were different. "So you felt transformed?" I asked.

Gia nodded. "Yes, changed in all sorts of ways."

"How?"

"I sense things, I feel things. I don't have the

words to explain it," Gia said. "It's like . . . you know when two wires touch? That spark. I feel that connection every day, all day long."

Gia tilted her head in the direction of the railroad tracks that ran alongside the river. "For example, I know that something is going to happen down there in a few minutes."

"A train?"

Gia nodded. "Soon. But it's not the kind of train that runs on a timetable. Most people don't know when these particular trains come or go."

She explained, "It will be tank cars carrying tar sands oil from Canada, or fracked oil from North Dakota," she said. "This oil is not like regular oil. It's highly, highly explosive, mixed with methane, propane, and other toxic chemicals.

"Those old tracks down there are rarely inspected. Many of the train cars that run on them aren't safe. Everybody knows it. Like soda cans on wheels . . . one accident and WHOOSH!"

"Has it ever happened?"

"Too many times," Gia answered. "In Virginia, fifty thousand gallons of crude spilled into the

James River and burned for two hours, a river of fire. Outside Quebec, massive fireballs incinerated part of a town. Thirty buildings melted into a thick, greasy mass. Cars burned like crumpled paper. Forty-seven people died, and five of those bodies were never found. They were vaporized by the sudden blast of radiant heat."

"Vaporized? What do you mean?" I asked.

"Poof, gone, like the spray out of a perfume bottle," Gia said. "This is truth I'm talking, Adrian. Facts."

"But how do you know all this stuff?" I asked.

"How do you *not* know it?" Gia countered. "It's my planet, I live here. Of course I know."

A light appeared in the distance. A long train came rolling down the old track. "Look," I pointed. Even in the dusky light, we could make out the general shape of the train. I even saw fluorescent yellow logos emblazoned on the side of each car: K & K CORP.

There's nothing like the vision of a train carving through the dark on steel rails. It was a beautiful sight, no matter what Gia said.

Gia lifted her chin to indicate the coming train. "The big oil companies make the profit, we take the risk." She counted the cars as they passed below us. "Thirteen, fourteen, fifteen . . . sixty-one, sixty-two . . . eighty-eight, eighty-nine, ninety . . ."

Suddenly sparks flew from the wheels as the front cars jumped the rails. We heard the grinding clash of metal on metal. The train rolled on like a serpent slithering out of the darkness. Somewhere inside an engineering droid sounded a horn and applied the brakes. This transpired a half mile away, hundreds of feet below us, but the shrill sounds vibrated through my body like a tuning fork. It happened so fast that neither of us uttered a word. We watched as smoke and sparks flew from the wheels.

And I realized: *This is it. This is what Gia wanted me to see.*

The train slowed and trembled to a halt. The first four cars had jumped the track, but they didn't topple over.

Nothing exploded.

In truth, nothing much happened at all until a few rescue trucks rolled up to survey the damage.

"That was close. If those cars had been damaged, people would have died." Gia clutched her stomach, as if she was experiencing a sharp pain.

"You knew this was going to happen."

Gia's face was ashen, her eyes glazed. Sweat beaded on her forehead.

"Are you okay?" I asked.

"I have to rest. I'm worn out, Adrian."

I helped her up and held her by the elbow as we headed down the hill. She felt frail in my arms, thin and weak. "I'll get you home on my bike," I said.

Gia nodded, not looking up. "I'm just so tired."

A NEW DAY,
A NEW ME

I guess you could say I asked for it.

It started when I complained to Zander about my stupid face. The typical grievances of the undead. Most days I didn't care what I looked like—or at least I learned how to unlive with it. I avoided mirrors, for example, and even papered over the one in the upstairs bathroom that Dane and I shared. But every once in a while I'd pass by a window or a shiny surface and catch my reflection looking back at me. It always gave me a start, as if I'd encountered a hideous stranger. The truth is, I sometimes forgot what I looked like. I felt . . . almost normal. But every time I caught a glimpse of my reflection, I instantly understood the physical revulsion that people experienced when they saw me. I felt it, too.

I was disgusting even to myself.

"You don't look so bad," Zander replied. "There are worse things, you know."

"I suppose," I said, unconvinced.

Zander stopped in his tracks. "What about people who are starving or kids who are sick in hospital beds? It's gotta suck, right? Think about it, Adrian. There are way worse things than being a zombie."

First Gia, now Zander. My friends were becoming less sympathetic to my situation.

"You know what you need?" Zander asked.

Uh-oh. I didn't like the sound of that.

"You need a makeover—and I know just the person who can do it. My cousin Clare. She's in tenth grade and knows all about that stuff. She wants to work in television as a makeup artist after high school. I'll hook you guys up."

"Wait, wait," I said. "I don't believe in—"

"Lighten up, Adrian. Clare's cool. She'll give you tips and pointers, find the colors that best suit you, that kind of stuff."

"The best colors?"

"It's a science—she's got a color wheel and everything. Who knows? Maybe she'll dye your hair purple, like Gia's."

"Not happening," I said. "I don't want a make-over. It's stupid."

Apparently Zander didn't hear that part, because the next afternoon he and a girl I'd never seen before were standing on my front stoop. "This is my cousin Clare, the one I told you about. Clare, this is Adrian."

I stood at the door, dumbstruck. This was not happening. The first thing I noticed about Clare was that she was big. Possibly the heaviest girl I'd seen in real life. I tried not to look at her body, so instead I focused on her eyes, which were welcoming and wide set. Hazel, I guess you'd call them.

"Are you going to let us in?" Zander asked.

"Oh yeah, sure."

Clare smelled faintly of lavender. "I'm glad to finally meet you. Zander talks about you all the time."

I glanced at Zander, who denied it with an embarrassed shake of his head.

Claire toted a small travel bag and said, "Are you ready for your makeover?"

I stammered, "I—um—"

"Listen, I'm gonna fly," Zander chimed in. "Probably better if I just leave you two alone." And before I knew it, my best friend was gone, good-bye. Clare breezed into our living room, set down her travel bag on the table, and asked, "Is here okay?"

"Yeah, sure, I mean, wait. Look, Clare—"

"Here, sit."

So I sat.

She opened her bag and began pulling out various jars, vials, brushes, and beauty supplies. "Let me look at you," Clare said. She gently placed two fingers under my chin, lifting it slightly, tilting it to and fro as she studied my face the way an artist might examine a painting. "First off, I have to say that you have amazing high cheekbones and a strong chin. I love your thick, spongy hair—I'm not going to touch it—the twists are brilliant. I kind of like the wild look. But what I really love is your forehead. It's a little larger than usual. Elegant, I think."

That surprised me. "Elegant? I've never heard that before."

"Oh yes," Clare said, still appraising my face. "Faces can be evenly divided into thirds. Up top, there's the forehead. The middle third goes from the eyebrows to the bottom of the nose. And the bottom third extends from the nose to the chin." She moved a flat hand in horizontal lines across her own face to demonstrate. "But in your case, I'd say that your forehead is more like forty percent—always a sign of nobility and intelligence."

I laughed. "Maybe I'm descended from kings."

Clare didn't take it as a joke. "Perhaps," she said, as if it might be true.

"Listen, Clare," I said. "You seem like a really nice person. I know that Zander asked you to come here today. But this isn't something—"

"I hear you," Clare interrupted. "Before you kick me out, let me explain that I don't believe in TV-version makeovers."

"You don't?"

"I hate them," Clare said emphatically. "Do you have AllAccessCable? There's, like, thirty-seven different makeover reality shows playing every week—and each one sells a lie. I blame Disney. It all goes back to *Cinderella*."

She took out a small sponge, dabbed something on it. "Do you mind?"

I decided to accept her help, since saying no didn't seem to be an option. Besides, I was curious about her problem with *Cinderella*.

"I can help you with skin care—taking care of yourself—most boys are horrible at that," she said. "Do you wash your face every night and every morning? Really scrub it?"

I closed my eyes and surrendered. "Tell me about *Cinderella*," I said.

"Well, it's also the Ugly Duckling complex, this idea that you can be transformed into something more beautiful—A NEW YOU!—and then everybody in the world will fall in love with you." As she worked on my skin, doing whatever it was that she did, Clare spoke in subdued tones, musical as a songbird. I listened, utterly relaxed.

"Every makeover show is the same," she stated. "Somebody comes on the show and the experts humiliate that person. Too overweight, too messy, too this, too that. Next: Surgery! Botox injections, makeup, hair extensions, teeth whitening, liposuction, cheek implants, a new butt, thinner eyebrows, and so it goes. At the end of the makeover, she doesn't look anything like herself. Next, friends and family are gathered for the big unveiling and, guess what, *everyone is amazed at the fabulous transformation!* They all clap and cheer. Then the transformed person comes onscreen with her fake lips like sofa pillows and fake hair and plastic boobs and talks to the camera."

"Yeah, that sounds about right," I said.

"The craziest part comes at the very end," Clare said. "She gushes that this new creation is somehow 'the real me'! More real than the old self she replaced."

I laughed. "Yeah, but how is that different from what you are doing here with me?"

"I'm not trying to turn you into somebody else," Clare said. "It's just common sense. I want to teach you how to take better care of your body—"

"Such as it is," I joked.

Clare shook her head, disapproving. "I can help with your outside appearance, but it's what's inside that counts. At least that's what I try to tell myself every day—despite what some people say."

I didn't know how to respond. I'd never met anyone like Clare before, who was smart and kind and also, I guess, still a little bit frightened. I understood her completely.

"You're not that overweight," I lied.

"*Ha!*" Clare laughed. "That's sweet of you to say. But honestly, Adrian, I'm just trying to be my best self."

She paused to write on a notepad. "I'm going to leave you with some instructions. And my number, if you need anything."

"Clare?"

"Yes?"

"How did you do it?"

"What do you mean?"

"You seem happy," I said. "Confident. I look at myself and I feel like such a loser."

Clare leaned forward, placing a manicured hand on my knee. "I got sick of it, as simple as that. Sick of hating myself. I finally realized that it's what's inside that matters." She tapped her chest twice. "The real me is inside."

"Yeah," I agreed.

"All those makeover shows have people looking outside for their happiness. The first phase is humiliation, followed by a shopping spree. Buying stuff, that's always the answer! You have to become your true self, Adrian, even if it's lonely sometimes." Clare abruptly stood and announced with a flourish, "Thus ends the sermon!"

"Do I owe you anything?" I asked. "That stuff must have cost a lot of money."

"No, no," she said, waving me off. "I get most of these products in school. Free trial samples, that kind of thing. Besides, you're Zander's friend. He's the best. I owe him a lot."

"Yeah, I guess I do, too," I said.

"By the way"—Clare waggled a finger toward the corner of the room—"you left your computer on. Bad idea. That's a waste of electricity."

I saw Clare out the door, thanked her again, and walked over to our big home computer. A red light indicated that it was on. Strange. I had a clear memory of turning it off. I'd been good about it ever since Talal had warned me: "They can activate all the cameras inside our computers." I sat down, staring at that red dot, frowning. I raised a fist at the screen and powered off. Better yet, I turned the whole computer around so that it faced the wall.

Have fun spying on that, creeps.

Upstairs, I tore the paper away from the mirror. To my surprise, I didn't look all that different; it was almost as if Clare hadn't done anything at all. My skin felt cleaner, refreshed maybe, but I was still the same old zombie me.

I wondered if I would ever learn to like the boy with sunken eyes who stared back at me in the mirror.

TIN MAN

Sunday night slowly rolled around. It had been one of those quiet, stay-at-home, do-nothing weekends. I tried not to think about Talal and the Bork brothers. Which, of course, was impossible. Had Tal figured out anything new? I'd ask him in school tomorrow.

"I know what I want to be for Halloween," Dane announced during dinner.

"Oh?" my mother said.

Dane gave a gnomish grin. "The Scarecrow from *The Wizard of Oz!*"

"Big surprise," I said.

"I need some old clothes, a hat, and some straw. Can we get straw, Mom?" Dane asked.

"Yes, that shouldn't be a problem. I think Olson's Farm sells hay bales this time of year."

"I need straw," Dane said, "not hay."

I explained, "It's the same thing, Dane. Hay, straw, there's no difference."

Dane's lower lip trembled. His eyes grew wet. "It's not the same," he argued. "I'm stuffed with straw, not hay. Mom?"

"It's okay, Dane, don't fret," my mother said. She shot a sour look in my direction, as if Dane's tears were somehow my fault. "I'll get you some straw. I promise."

"Thanks," Dane said, instantly cheering up. "Which character do you want to be on Halloween, Adrian?"

"Um? What?"

"If I'm the Scarecrow, you can be the Cowardly Lion or the Tin Man. We'll have to find a girl to be Dorothy. Do you know any girls?"

"Slow down a sec, Dane. What are you talking about?"

He seemed especially fragile this morning, a china teacup that had to be handled ever so gently. My little brother, the person who loved me most of all, said, "I want to paint our front bricks yellow. Then we can go trick-or-treating together."

"I'm in middle school, Dane," I explained. "I'm not really into getting dressed up for Halloween."

"Why not?"

"It's just, I don't know . . ." I shrugged. I didn't really have an answer to that one. I knew there must be an end point when we'd all grow up and stop ringing doorbells, but I didn't know exactly when that time would come. Was this the year I'd have to give up trick-or-treating? Maybe I could still do it a little bit, on the down low, as long as I didn't act too *into* it. Ring a bell, mumble something, and look bored.

Dane stared at me in disbelief, as if I'd just announced that pizza was illegal. He powered on. "Your friend Zander could be the Cowardly Lion.

He's chubby, and I think the Lion should be sort of soft in the middle, don't you think?"

"I guess," I replied.

"So that makes you the Tin Man," Dane said. "No heart."

I looked across the table at my mother. No help there.

"Dane, I don't know . . . ," I said.

"You have to," he insisted.

My mother cleared her throat. "We can discuss it later, Dane. There's still time before Halloween."

Dane glanced at me as if I'd just stabbed him in the back with a fork. "Just forget it," he muttered.

"Dane—" I faltered. "Let me think about it, okay?"

He didn't look up, didn't say a word, but I saw his face relax a little.

"I might know a good Dorothy," I offered. "If you don't mind purple hair."

That elicited the smile I needed to see. "Really? Who?" he asked.

"This girl I know. I'll ask her."

The truth was, I used to love Halloween. Free candy, right? But these days I felt uneasy. Little-boy games were behind me. What would everybody else think if they saw me? I wasn't sure what to do anymore. I'd have to check with my friends. It was like there was a new rule book for kids my age, but no one had a copy of it. We all had to make it up as we limped along.

To make things even more horrible, there was a rumor in school that some sixth graders were going dressed up as, you guessed it, zombies. More specifically: me. I can't say I was psyched about that. I imagined a bunch of kids walking around dressed as me. As if my entire existence were some kind of holiday joke. Gee, no thanks.

I cut into my steak. It was pink inside, and blood dripped onto my plate. For some reason it angered me. "I asked for raw," I complained.

"You said rare," my mother replied. "I'm sorry if I cooked it too long. I'm sure it's just fine."

"It's not fine." I felt agitated, my temper rising. More and more, I craved raw meat. "You shouldn't have cooked it at all. It's not how I like it!" I pounded my fist on the table. Cutlery rattled, plates bounced. A drinking glass toppled and shattered.

"Adrian!" My mother stood, frightened. "What is going on with you? Put that down."

I realized that I still had the bloody steak knife in my hand. Was my own mother afraid of me? "I just want food the way I like it, that's all. Is that too much to ask?"

"I can't give you uncooked meat," she argued. "You'll get sick. It's not right. It's not . . . normal."

"That's what you want, isn't it?" I blurted. "A normal kid. Too bad you're stuck with me!"

I climbed the stairs to my room and slammed the door. Nobody tried to coax me out. No soft words at the door, no whispered forgiveness. I rolled over on my bed and placed a hand over my chest. I waited for some sound, a vibration, a thump. Something, anything. All I received was echoing silence. I remembered the Tin Man squeaking in his feeble voice, "Oil can, oil can."

I felt alone, an outcast in my own home.

My stomach rumbled.

For the first time since the accident, I felt hungry.

CROWS

Crows are nature's trash collectors. But nobody gives them credit for a job well done. Imagine this:

Some fat squirrel, hopped up on a bellyful of acorns, sluggishly moves across the pavement just as an SUV barrels down the road.

SPLAT!

It is not a pretty sight, right? Most folks see that and think—*ew!* Road kill, smashed squirrel, bloody mess flattened near the curb.

This kind of thing happens all the time. The car's tire represents the circle of life. Believe me, the statistics on flattened squirrels would break your heart, assuming you had one. The good news: It's not a problem! (Except for the squashed squirrels, naturally.) You'd think we'd have dead squirrels piled up all over town. Stacks and stacks of them. But that's where the crows and vultures come in. They love dead squirrels! For these carrion eaters, it's fine dining with a faint aftertaste of rubber.

CROW #1: "Look, here comes an SUV."
CROW #2: "Come on, baby! Daddy's starving!"
   SCREECH, SPLAT!
CROW #1: "Yes! Flattened!"
CROW #2: "Let's eat!"

When something's dead, normally it would be unpleasant to look at. Over time, the carcass would become a breeding ground for festering diseases, white maggots, all sorts of creepy stuff. Bad news for you and me. Fortunately, crows can't get enough carrion! They love dining on dead animals and, in the process, making our lives a lot better by tidying up.

So I say, "Come on, everybody. Let's give a long slow clap for our friends the crows and vultures." *Clap, clap, clap.*

As a semi-dead seventh-grader, I'm glad those crows haven't come after me. Good thing my little brother is a part-time scarecrow. I remembered the recent sight of vultures swirling overhead. Maybe I wasn't so safe after all.

Today I found a dead squirrel outside my house. A fresh kill, blood still leaking from its nose, but otherwise not too shabby. I prodded it with my foot. I glanced up the road, down the road. No one in sight. Just me and that squirrel.

Do I dare? Or do I dare?

I stepped away, horrified.

What was happening to me?

What was I becoming?

I knew that middle school would be a time of changes, but I thought that would be like, I don't know, my voice getting deeper. A breakout of back acne or something. But this was ridiculous. I was literally thinking about scarfing up a dead squirrel from the street.

Then I stopped thinking altogether.

Some other, deeper instinct told me what to do.

Moments later, I dragged a sleeve across my mouth and fled into the house, my back to the street.

WORKING
THE CASE

"Any progress on the case?" I asked Talal.

We were sitting in a downtown laundromat, amid rows of rattling washers and dryers. It was Talal's idea of a relatively safe place from drones and eavesdroppers. Only two people were inside, a red-haired woman in a rumpled sweater, an e-cigarette dangling from her lip, who carried in three trash bags full of clothes. She went about her routine as if she'd been there before, giving us only the briefest once-over when we entered. A man sat in a chair, his long legs extended, black work boots untied. He was staring, transfixed, into the glass circle of a dryer as clothes tumbled round and round. His hair was uncombed, and a thin scar ran from the corner of his mouth to his chin. He muttered to himself without ever, it seemed, so much as glancing our direction.

"I'm following a few leads, but—" Talal shrugged, suddenly silent.

"You think it's safe to talk here?" I asked.

Talal scanned the laundromat once more. He lifted his hands helplessly as if to say, *Who knows.*

"So? Anything at all?" I asked.

"You've read up on them, right?"

"Yeah, I did my homework. But for such powerful men, there's not a lot of information out there."

Talal nodded. "They like to stay clear of the spotlight. So tell me," he said, "what's the one thing about Kalvin and Kristoff Bork that sticks out to you?"

I thought it over. I wanted to say something insightful, impress Talal with my piercing intelligence. I didn't feel too confident. "Well, for starters, they are unbelievably rich. *Forbes* listed them as the two richest men in the world. They donate a lot of money to causes they care about, sometimes to genuinely good charities. Mostly they pour millions of dollars into helping certain politicians win elections."

Talal nodded. "That's correct. In return, congressmen, judges, and senators owe the Bork brothers a favor or two. That's how the world works."

"Yeah, I guess the Borks expect them to look out for the interests of K & K if any new laws come up for a vote in the House or the Senate," I agreed. "The Borks know that if they buy enough important friends, they can control things. They don't want the government regulating their businesses, and they don't want to lose profits by worrying about the environment. The Borks will do anything to stop alternative energies from gaining support in Washington, D.C."

"Yeah, yeah, they tilt at windmills," Talal mused. "They don't want the world to change for the better. It's not in their short-term interest—they make billions every year by using our sky as an open sewer. But you're missing the obvious thing."

I gave him a blank look.

"There are almost no photographs," Talal said.

"Shy, I guess."

Talal pulled a rumpled paper from his pocket. It showed a blurry photograph of the Bork brothers, as if taken from a great distance. "This is one of the rare shots. Look at them," he insisted.

The brothers were nearly identical, with gaunt faces, thin lips, and slicked-back hair. Their heads were close together, as if the camera had captured them at the moment when one brother had whispered into the other's ear. I still wasn't getting it.

The front door opened, and a deeply tanned man in a cream-colored suit entered, carrying a black pillowcase full of laundry. He rolled past a half-dozen empty machines and slapped down a handful of quarters on a washer near us. "My damn washer at home is on the fritz," he grumbled. "You're not planning on using this one, are you boys?"

"Nope," Talal replied. "We're already gone."

"Don't leave on my account."

"No worries," Talal said, preparing to leave. I pulled the hoodie over my head and shuffled out.

The man held his phone in his hand. He punched out a text and maybe, just possibly, snapped a photo as we passed.

"They're everywhere," Talal said as we hit the sidewalk.

"You think he works for them?"

"He had long hair covering his ears," Talal said. "Most of the time, a guy in an expensive suit like that wears his hair cropped short."

"So?"

"So with long hair he can easily hide a transmitting device in his ears," Talal said. "Plus, rich guys in suits like that call in repairmen. They don't do laundromats, it's beneath them. And I didn't like the way he intentionally picked a washer that was close to us. It didn't feel right."

"You might be a little paranoid," I said.

Talal laughed. "Just because I'm paranoid doesn't mean they're not out to get us." We continued walking outside a strip of stores. Talal spoke in his normal voice, for the present time not worrying about being overheard. "My father is a surgeon. He told me that in medical school they taught him that when he makes a diagnosis, he should always think of something called Occam's razor. Have you ever heard of it?"

"I don't shave," I said, once again feeling dim-witted in his company.

"Basically, if you hear the sound of hooves coming up behind you, think horses, not zebras," Talal said. "Get it? Most times, the simplest answer is the correct one."

I thought of the lack of photographs. "Ah, the Bork brothers are—"

"Not so loud," Talal warned.

"—hiding something," I whispered.

Talal yanked me by the arm and took a sharp right turn into a coffee shop. We stood near the espresso machine, which hummed and whirred and gurgled with a terrible racket. "Yeah," he agreed. "They are hiding something."

"Okay, but what does it have to do with me?"

Talal purchased two large chocolate chip cookies and a couple of drinks. He found a table located directly under a stereo speaker. Electronica music, all blips and drum machines, pulsed at distracting volumes. Talal cupped a hand around his mouth and said, "If we talk softly, I doubt they can record our voices in all this noise."

I gave him a thumbs-up.

"Let's back up a minute," Tal began. "The Borks made money all their lives. Gobs of it. Oil, real estate, hotels, hedge funds, what have you. But they got crazy rich when they became data collectors."

"Okay, I give up," I said, waving my hands. "What's a data collector?"

"Do you want the long answer or the short one?"

"I want you to explain it as if you're talking to a stuffed meerkat," I said, grinning.

"Gotcha," Talal said. "Okay, the core of the K & K business is collecting information on people. They were the ones who figured it out first. We live in a digital age. Information is gold. Then they sell that information to other, smaller businesses. For example, one day you go on a website and click on a sneaker you like. You don't buy it, you just look. You are thinking about it. Daydreaming. The next day, an advertisement for that same sneaker pops up on your phone. That evening, outside your bedroom window, a hologram image of that same sneaker scampers across the night sky. How did they know?" he asked. "It's all data collection. Numbers, algorithms, computers. The day you clicked on that sneaker, the Borks put a target on your back."

"It all connects," I murmured. "We've been so stupid."

"What?"

"Just something Gia said," I replied. "*It all connects.* We began by asking the wrong question. You asked me what's the one thing about Kalvin and Kristoff Bork that sticks out? Occam's razor, remember? The obvious thing. We should have been asking that question about *me*."

Tal understood immediately. He leaned forward on his elbows. "You're right, Adrian. You're the key to this mystery, not them. And what makes you so special? You are the zombie boy who somehow survives without a beating heart. You should not exist, and yet here you are." He chomped into his cookie. "If I had ten balloons, I'd bet every single one that the Bork brothers are dying to know how you do it."

A feeling of dread sank in my stomach like a bad burrito. I looked away, lost in thought.

"What are you thinking, Adrian?"

"I want to meet them," I decided.

"The Bork brothers?" Talal raised his eyebrows, pushed the fedora back on his head. "Not easy. They are very reclusive."

"You said they don't live too far from here. Less than an hour away," I insisted.

"It's not like we can knock on their door like we're selling Girl Scout cookies," Talal said.

"True," I agreed. "But you'll think of something."

HIVE MIND

Zander persuaded Gia and me to attend the first meeting of a new school club, the Animal Protection Society, set to take place at the beehive in the organic garden out back. Zander was so excited about the meeting, we couldn't refuse. Talal begged off, citing medical reasons. He claimed he was allergic to after-school activities.

"Are you worried about bee stings?" I asked Gia. "I mean, you know—"

Gia grinned. "That's not a problem anymore.

Besides, Ms. Fjord says it's highly unlikely the bees would sting us, as long as we don't do anything stupid."

We met Zander at his locker. "Until yesterday, I had no idea we even had a hive on school grounds," Gia said. "It's so cool."

"I know, right?" Zander agreed, bobbing his head as we pushed open the back doors. The day was exceptionally clear and warm for mid-October. The leaves on the trees put on their brightest colors, and the warm sun shone down on our heads.

"Gorgeous day, I love it!" Gia exclaimed. She stretched her arms out and performed balletic twirls on the grass. Gia appeared fully recovered from the sharp pains that had crippled her during the train derailment.

"Beekeeping is Ms. Fjord's hobby," Zander explained. "When she got hired at school over the summer, she offered to bring one of her hives here."

"Isn't it dangerous?" I asked.

"Nah," Zander said. "Just don't do anything stupid to agitate the bees, and they'll leave you alone."

"Okay, I'll try not to be stupid."

Gia patted me on the shoulder. "Good luck with that, pal."

Ms. Fjord was already working in the garden, dressed in jeans, bright rubber gloves, and a floppy sun hat. When she saw us approach, Ms. Fjord smiled brightly and gave a huge, hearty wave across the field, as if we were a passing airplane and she'd been stranded for weeks on an inflatable raft. I half expected her to shoot off a flare gun.

"Is it just us?" Gia asked Zander. "We're the entire Animal Protection Society?"

"The club's just starting out," Zander said. "It'll grow, you'll see. People will wake up." Zander pushed ahead to greet Ms. Fjord.

"Wow, I've never seen that before," I observed. "Zander's literally running."

"*Literally* running?" Gia asked, arching an eyebrow. "As opposed to figuratively running?"

"Don't get all grammatical with me," I said, cuffing her on the shoulder.

Gia grinned back, large eyes beaming.

Ms. Fjord had an energy that made her talk in

exclamation points. She flashed a toothy smile. "I'm so glad you've come to meet our bees!"

I couldn't locate the hive until she pointed out where it stood, tucked in the far corner of the garden. The hive looked like a rectangular wooden box, nothing fancy, about four feet high.

"Come," she said. "We're lucky it's a warm day, so the bees are still active. I'm not going to show you the inside of the frame today. It's best if we do that in the spring."

I didn't complain. I wasn't super eager to get up close and personal with thousands of bees.

"How do they survive during the winter?" Gia asked.

"Well, it's really interesting," Ms. Fjord said. "They don't hibernate; instead, the colony will huddle together in a ball to keep warm. Have you seen the movie *The March of the Penguins*? It's like that. Here in the northeast, where winters are really cold, the colony will form a huddle that's the size of a basketball."

"And the queen bee is in the center of it," Zander added.

Ms. Fjord pointed out the holes at the bottom of the box. "When the bees are getting ready to overwinter, I add these metal guards to keep out mice and other animals that might want to burrow inside. And here"—she pointed to two sides of the box—"I've added black tar paper on the southern and eastern exposures to help absorb heat from the sun. On the other two sides, I've attached insulation."

"How many bees are in a hive?" Gia asked.

"About fifty thousand is a healthy number," Ms. Fjord replied.

If I could whistle halfway decently, I would have done it.

Ms. Fjord explained that during pollination season she liked to sit in a lawn chair about ten feet away from the hive, just watching them come and go. "I don't like to disturb them, and I can learn a lot about the health of the hive just by observing the activity. Some days I'll sit out with a cup of Lemon Zinger and a book. Or I'll close my eyes and contemplate the stillness—this awesome, mysterious world."

She looked directly at me when she said those last four words: *this awesome, mysterious world.*

"That sounds so nice," Gia said.

"It is, I love it!" Ms. Fjord gushed, turning to Gia. "Come place your ear against the side. Can you hear anything?"

Gia's eyes brightened, and she let out a startled gasp. "Yes, a hum!"

Ms. Fjord laughed. "We'll turn you into a bee-keeper yet!"

She continued: "During the winter, there's not much work for a beekeeper. The bees need enough honey to survive, and some keepers like to give them sugar water. I'll come by to listen once a month, to make sure the hive is in good health. Maybe I just miss them!" she said with a laugh. "The real work begins in the spring. You can help me then, if you'd like."

"Sure, that'd be great." Gia seemed relaxed and happy to soak up the natural world. It struck me that she seemed more vibrant in the garden, like a plant after a soft rain, as if she derived energy from the nearness of the hive.

We learned some interesting facts, too. Mostly from Zander, who specialized in rattling off that kind of data.

"I didn't know you were such a bee expert," I said to Zander, hoping he might take the hint.

"Oh yes," Ms. Fjord interjected. "Zander might even start his own hive, isn't that right?"

Zander looked down in embarrassment. "Maybe. I hope so."

Ms. Fjord told us that Zander was writing an essay to submit to a Young Beekeeper contest. "The winner gets a starter kit as a prize."

"Seriously? That's awesome, Zander," Gia said.

"You think so?" he asked.

"Oh yes," Gia affirmed.

I asked Ms. Fjord how she got into beekeeping. She said, "Well, let me see. I started reading about how honeybees were mysteriously disappearing. I don't know why, but it really hit me. I just figured that maybe I could do something to help. I mean, bees are super important to the food chain. I'm just one person, but I wanted to do something. What I didn't expect was how much I would end up loving my bees. I went from one hive, to two hives, then four, eight—now I'm up to sixteen hives. My husband and I sell honey at the farmers' market. I make beeswax candles and sell them, too."

It was a great day, simply hanging out and talking in the garden with Ms. Fjord. This sounds dumb, but out there it felt like we were all equals. Ms. Fjord was a cheerful, natural person, and she didn't talk down to us. I liked seeing her out of the classroom, where she could be more herself. I glanced around: Zander couldn't stop smiling, and Gia looked downright inspired, like she might spontaneously burst with happiness. For the first time in a long time, I let my own problems drift away, as if I were releasing my grip from a string to watch a helium balloon rise slowly into the atmosphere. Smaller, smaller, smaller . . . until the great blue sky swallowed it whole. Maybe things would turn out okay for me after all. Out here in the garden, for a few minutes at least, hope felt possible.

DARYL BITES BACK

"Hey, Chubby Bubbles!"

Zander and I were climbing the main stairs to school at that bleary hour before any self-respecting student is fully awake. The familiar voice came from behind us. "Ignore him, keep walking," I advised Zander.

"Chubby! You're not just fat, you're deaf, too? Hold up a minute! I've got to tell you something," Daryl called. "You too, gimp."

Zander stopped and turned. "What's your problem, Northrup?"

Daryl smirked, taking pleasure in Zander's irritation. Daryl leaned back, putting a hand over his heart. "I don't have a problem. I feel freaking awesome. But I'm worried about your dopey beehive. I've seen you back there, right?"

I stood shoulder to shoulder with my friend. "What have you done, Daryl?"

Daryl smiled, feigning innocence. "Who, me?"

Talal joined us, glancing from face to face. "Is everybody okay?"

"Geez, nice hat," Daryl remarked. "You buy it at a garage sale for midget hipsters?"

"Good one," Talal remarked. "I'll have to write that down."

"Just answer my question, Daryl," I demanded. "What have you done?"

"I haven't done nothing. I'm just telling you what I saw," Daryl said. He glared at me, and I could see that the old fearlessness had returned. He placed a large hand on Zander's shoulder, leaned in, and whispered, ever so softly, "I was just wondering why it was all smashed up. You know? Who even brings bees onto school grounds anyway?"

Zander pushed Daryl's hand away.

Daryl returned it to Zander's shoulder. "Try that again, you gutless tub of jelly."

Zander didn't move.

"Didn't think so," Daryl scoffed.

"Come on, forget him." I pulled Zander away. "Let's check the hive."

The three of us—Zander, Talal, and I—circled around the back of the school. "We'll be a few minutes late, but so what," I said.

As we drew closer to the garden, Zander let out a muffled, "Oh no."

The entire hive had been knocked over. Some boxes and frames had fallen out, possibly broken. When I moved to rush forward, Zander grabbed my arm. "Don't get too close," he warned. "The bees are going to be all stirred up. They'll be aggressive."

We stood there helplessly, three boys in a field, unsure of what to do. "Guys," Talal said. He stepped toward the school, gesturing. "We can't deal with this now."

I nodded to Zander. "He's right."

"It had to be Daryl, right?" Zander said, uttering

an inspired string of curses. "How could anybody do that?"

"Oh, it was him, all right," Talal said. "Didn't you see that red welt on his wrist? I'd bet ten balloons it's a bee sting."

Most of the school day was scheduled for standardized tests. Fortunately, we had a few minutes to break the news to Ms. Fjord in her classroom. She moved to the corner window and craned her neck. From that vantage point, we could barely make out the garden in the distance. "How bad?" she asked.

"We don't know," Zander answered. "I didn't want to get too near."

"Right, right," she said, "that's good, Zander. They'll be angry for a couple of days. I'll have to notify the principal, warn students to steer clear. Let's see, um . . ."

She seemed uncertain, almost dazed. She walked unsteadily to her chair and sat down.

"Water?" I asked, lifting one of her empty coffee mugs.

She sat blinking, thoughts still elsewhere. "Oh yes, please. Thank you, Adrian."

After a few minutes, Ms. Fjord collected herself. She made a plan with Zander. "We'll have to leave them alone for a few days," she said. "Then on, um"— she checked the desk calendar; it was Thursday, two days before Halloween—"on Sunday morning, I'll have to put on some protective gear to assess the damage."

"I want to help," Zander offered.

"Me too," I said.

Ms. Fjord's smile flickered. "It will be all right," she said with new resolve. "Bees have been around for millions of years. Hives have survived bear attacks in the past, and our hive will survive this, too. It's all just so disheartening. I can't believe someone would do that."

"Do you think they'll swarm?" Zander wondered.

"No, bees aren't likely to swarm in October," Ms. Fjord replied. "That's more of a late-spring to midsummer event. If the hive gets too crowded, part of the colony will swarm to establish a new hive. I just hope the queen is all right."

"What if she's not?" Zander asked. "What if she got crushed?"

"If that's the case, we'll have to find a new queen, and quickly. This time of year, I can always order one by mail from a large apiary." She looked up, saw the concern on Zander's face. "We're lucky it's been unseasonably warm—I guess climate change has its benefits. If it were freezing, we might have lost the entire hive."

An announcement came over the loudspeaker, informing us that it was time to proceed to our testing locations. We knew the routine by heart. Like robots, all the students filed out, sharpened pencils in our fists. We were programmed to color in answer bubbles.

ZANDER'S REVENGE

School had kept us busy all week with one of its notorious "test clusters." Every day we were forced to take a brutal battery of standardized tests. By Thursday, today, we were tired and stressed. Weirdly, our teachers kept reassuring us that these tests didn't matter and would not even be graded, because they were just practice tests for the upcoming *real* tests—on which our lives depended, or so we were led to believe. It was confusing.

Earlier that week, Ms. Fjord had muttered that the tests represented "a triumph of mindless bureaucracy over common sense." I wasn't sure what she meant, but I could tell she felt these tests were a waste of time, money, and minds.

Long columns of desks, twelve across, thirty-five deep, had been set up in the huge gymnasium to squeeze in more than four hundred test-takers at one time. We sat obediently, like factory workers in some bizarre futuristic world, and filled in answer bubbles with No. 2 pencils. The only sounds came from the heels of proctors walking up and down the rows, along with assorted sighs and pitiful groans from the students, and the *scratch-scratch-scratch*ing of graphite pencils on paper. We sat there slumped over, spittle trickling from our mouths, eyes glazed, minds numbed. When the bell rang, we were given thirty minutes to eat before we had to return for the next round of testing. (They had to let us eat, according to the rules of the Geneva convention.)

Our lunch table had grown to include me, Zander, Talal, and Gia. I filled in Gia about our recent run-in with Daryl. "He's getting aggressive," I said. "I'm worried about what he's going to do next."

"I have an idea," Zander offered.

All eyes turned to him.

"It seems to me that Daryl isn't afraid of Adrian anymore," he reasoned. "After the showdown outside the pizza place, Daryl was pretty shaken up. He didn't know what to think."

I smiled. "Well, I did threaten him."

"For real?" Talal asked, obviously impressed. "You threatened Daryl?"

Gia laughed. "He said, 'Get out of here now or I'll blankety-blank eat your braaaiiins!'"

I shrugged helplessly. "I don't know, it just popped out of my mouth."

"You should have been there, Tal," Gia said. "Adrian was fantastic!"

"Yes, he was," Zander agreed. "Daryl couldn't back off fast enough."

We all roared, drawing looks from the other tables.

"Seriously, though," Zander said, "a lot of people were scared of Adrian back then. Now weeks have passed, and Adrian hasn't done anything the least bit scary. The fear has washed away."

"Yesterday, Lydia Gregovich told me that Adrian is cute," Gia added.

"Oooooh, Zombie Boy and Lydia, getting tight," Talal joked.

"That's my point," Zander spoke up. "Adrian is starting to fit in again, and Daryl is back to being Daryl, the worst human being on the planet. Adrian humiliated Daryl in front of his friends. Now Daryl wants revenge."

Gia nodded. "Agreed. So what's your plan?"

Zander glanced right and left. He leaned forward. "We'll do it after the dance Friday night . . ."

At the end, we shook hands on it.

Gia said, "Let's nail this creep once and for all."

MAN WITH A THIN WHITE SCAR

"We've still got that other thing to worry about," Talal said by the recycling bins. "Our friends the Borks. I think today's the day. Are you still sure you want to meet them?"

I glanced at Gia. If she knew the future, she wasn't saying.

"Yeah, sure, I'm sure," I said. "But I still don't see how we're going to pull this off."

Talal grinned, blew on his fingernails. "That's

why I get paid the big bucks." He told me to meet him outside the cemetery front gate on Grove Street at four o'clock sharp.

My nervous excitement grew as the day progressed. It wasn't a happy kind of feeling, like the anticipation of a birthday party or holiday celebration. It was more like the anxious dread I imagine an actor might experience before taking the stage. A sense that something big was about to happen. I was going to meet the Bork brothers. It made me want to hurl.

That afternoon, Principal Rouster interrupted testing for an important announcement.

Kkccchh. Kkccchh. Tap-tap. TAP-TAP. "Wait, what?—Is this thing on?" *SQUAAAWWWKK— whirr—kkccchh.* "Good afternoon, Nixon Middle School!"

We all groaned. . . .

"I've got some more really bad news," Principal Rouster announced. "There's been flooding in the south wing. Therefore, we've once again been forced to halt all water operations.

"In addition, I wish to address rumors about

this Friday's Halloween dance. The rumors are par-
tially true. There will, in fact, be a Halloween
dance this Friday."

A chorus of excited cheers, mostly from the
girls, erupted throughout the school.

"However," Principal Rouster stated, "the rumors
are incorrect on several significant points. One,
this is NOT—I repeat, NOT—a couples dance. No
student is allowed to bring a date to the dance.
Two, there will be no slow dancing. Three, there
will be no public displays of affection. This includes
hand-holding, hugging, high-fiving, fist-bumping,
and booty-shaking. If anyone is the least bit friendly
to each other, you will be immediately escorted out
of the building.

"What a fun night it'll be!" Principal Rouster
clucked.

Sigh. We really were just inmates in an asylum.
My friends and I had big plans for the night of the
dance, but I couldn't allow myself to think about it.
First I had to get through this test, then cut a deal
with the Bork brothers.

After school, I pedaled furiously to meet Talal as instructed.

"Why all the way out here?" I complained, climbing off my bicycle.

"Clear site lines." Talal looked up. The sky was gray and empty except for one bird circling high overhead. Talal smiled. "Plus, we had to get away from people."

He sat cross-legged on the grass and leaned against the iron fence that bordered the cemetery. I locked my bike and joined him.

"I still don't get it," I said. "How are we getting there?"

Talal tapped an index finger against his forehead. "Tell me again why you want to talk to the Bork brothers."

I was confused. "You already know, Tal."

"Tell me again, Adrian Lazarus," he repeated.

It was bizarre to hear him address me by my full name. His eyes fixed me with a strange stare.

Talal gave a slight nod, as if trying to send a silent signal.

I said, "Okay, well, I figured they might be interested in working out a deal . . ."

"Louder," Talal said. "And don't tell me, tell them." He pointed to the bird circling in the sky. "Nice and clear, so the little birdie can catch every word."

I gazed up at the black speck hovering in the sky, wings perfectly still.

Another drone?

Fifteen minutes later, a long black limousine pulled up next to us. The passenger window slid down and the driver leaned toward us. "I understand you gentlemen might need a ride," he said.

I recognized the man's face, even under the chauffeur's hat, and the thin white scar that ran from the corner of his lip. He produced a card, which he offered with an outstretched hand. Talal stood to brush the grass from his coat. He moved with exaggerated slowness, refusing to be rushed. He finally plucked the card from the man's hand and, without so much as a glance, tucked it into the deep pocket of his trench coat.

"My mother told me never to get into cars with strangers," he demurred.

The stone-faced driver nodded. "Your mother is wise. But I'm not exactly a stranger. We've met before."

"You were at the laundromat," I said.

The man studied my face for a long moment. "So you're the one, huh? Amazing." He tipped his cap. "My employers are ready to meet you."

The driver's-side door opened and he emerged, standing tall and erect in a black suit. He walked around the car, gave us a slight bow, and opened the back door.

"Sweet ride," Talal observed. "You got anything to eat in there? Or are we going to stop at the drive-thru for a bucket of instant chicken?"

The driver did not share Talal's sense of humor. He gestured me inside with a tilt of his head.

"What's your name?" I asked.

He showed no expression. "My name is unimportant."

"Pleased to meet you, Unimportant," I deadpanned. "My name is—"

"Lazarus, the boy who rose again," he said. "My employers are quite familiar with your case history."

It shouldn't have surprised me to hear those words, but they still caused a tremor of unease to ripple down my spine. I wondered if I was making a mistake. Too late. Something told me that eventually I'd have to come face-to-face with the notorious Bork brothers. If I could help them in some way, maybe they could do something for me. I couldn't allow them to follow me around forever. Besides, I'd never been in a stretch limousine before. I admired the black leather interior and the car's overall vibe of wealth, taste, and luxury. Talal was busy exploring every nook and cranny, pushing buttons, sliding out drawers, opening secret compartments. I declined his offer of salted cashews, malted milk balls, and K & K Kola.

Talal took a swig and burped loudly.

"You'll find that the car is fully appointed with refreshments to suit your taste. My employers wish to extend every courtesy," the driver said. He shut the door and returned to his seat behind the wheel. "Make yourselves at home. They will be expecting you within the hour." He gazed back at us in the rearview mirror, as if awaiting some signal.

Talal found the stereo system, tuned in a station on satellite, and pumped up the volume, huge. "Boom," he said, clapping his hands together. "I like it—I like it a lot. You good with this, Adrian?"

"I'm good. Let's do it."

"We're off to see the wizard," Talal announced, and at those words, the luxury car eased into the lane as if sailing soundlessly on white, puffy clouds.

KRISTOFF AND KALVIN

We rolled up the long, winding driveway to the massive white mansion at the top of the hill. Talal whistled at the sight of it. "Ah, now this is a horse of a different color," he murmured.

Talal elbowed me. The lift of his chin directed my attention to the far side of the estate. The area was crowded with construction materials of every sort, including scaffolding, cement mixers, heavy-duty forklifts, Bobcats, and stacks of lumber.

"What are they building over there?" Talal asked.

As our driver turned his head in reply, I could once again make out his thin white scar. "I don't get paid to ask questions," he said, without really providing an answer.

"How long have you worked for the Bork brothers?" I asked.

"Years," he replied.

"Do you like it?"

"I'm well paid."

"And how about the Borks?" Talal asked. "Do you like them?"

The driver said, "I can't say one way or the other."

"No opinion?" Talal asked.

"I've never met them, to be perfectly honest with you," the driver said.

"Excuse me? Never?" Talal said. I could hear the surprise in his voice.

"They don't go out much. Besides, I'm just an errand boy, glad to have a job. So that's enough chitchat outta me." At those words, the car rolled to a stop and automatically shifted into park. Our guide stepped out to open the door for us. "I'll be here, cooling my heels," he informed us. "I'll give you a lift back home when you're ready."

An unsmiling man waited for us at the main door. He was thickset, built like a bank vault, and he held up a hand the size of a dinner plate. "Not you," he growled at Talal.

"Nuh-uh, that wasn't the deal," Talal protested.

The bodyguard—he *must* have been a bodyguard, though he could have worked as a professional wrestler on weekends—took one step forward. He did a pretty good impression of a brick wall.

"It's okay, I'll be all right," I spoke up, hoping it was true. "You can wait here, Tal."

"You sure?"

"Sure, I'm sure," I lied, forcing a smile to my face. It wasn't like we had a choice. The man gestured with a slow sweep of his arm, thick as a fence post. Talal sat on the front steps, rolling his hat around an extended index finger. The door clicked shut behind him.

I was inside, and I was on my own.

The bodyguard led the way. We went through a huge tiled lobby, through a set of locked double doors, up a wide flight of carpeted stairs, and down another hallway.

About twenty feet ahead, a door opened and a tall blond woman in a nurse's uniform stepped into the hallway. She seemed startled to see us there, as if she hadn't expected to be seen, and quickly retreated into the room from which she'd come.

"Who's that?" I asked.

"No one," the bodyguard helpfully explained.

Sigh. I'd met kitchen appliances with more personality.

As I stood wondering about the nurse I'd just seen—*What was she doing here? Was someone sick?*—the bodyguard opened the door to my right. "This way," he said.

I stepped into a green room. It was dimly lit—long and narrow and high-ceilinged. *Click*, the door shut behind me. The guard took his position beside it, his feet wide, his hands clasped together, his face as blank as slate.

"Come forward!" boomed a deep, resonant voice.

Lights flickered at the far end of the room, at least one hundred feet away. Floor-length drapes, the plum-dark color of avocado skin, covered the windows. Wall sconces gave off a greenish glow. In fact, I realized that most everything in the room was a shade of green—the walls, the faint lights, even the carpet. I walked, a little unsteadily, toward the voice. As I drew closer, the dark forms became clear. A few carpeted steps led to a sort of high table, or altar, at the end of the room. I stood at the bottom of those steps, looking up at an enormous television screen that filled the entire wall. Two huge, wizened heads floated on the screen. Their images were grainy, as if the signal were being sent from another world, with the flickering snow of an ancient tube television from the 1960s. The faces were wrinkled, gnarled, and shriveled.

Wisps of smoke billowed up from somewhere. Lights flashed and danced, causing me to shield my eyes.

"I am Kristoff Bork," boomed the face on the right. His voice was loud and intimidating. It sounded amplified and unreal. "And this is my dear brother, Kalvin Bork."

Kalvin's face twitched, a grimace of recognition, but otherwise remained expressionless, heavy-lidded, and feeble.

I hesitated. *Was I really speaking to faces on a television screen?* "My name is—"

"Silence," Kristoff interrupted. "We know who you are, Adrian Lazarus."

The lights in the room pulsed brighter, as if lit by Kristoff's anger.

"We are old men," Kristoff said, his tone softer, his eyes twinkling. The lights dimmed. "But you—and you alone—hold the secret to eternal life."

Coming here had been a serious mistake. My brain was flooded with noise and confusion. "What do you want from me?" I asked.

Kristoff glanced to the side, his lips tightened to a thin line. He nodded once.

A door opened and shut from somewhere behind

the screen. A man in a white lab coat entered the room. "Dr. Halpert!" I said in astonishment.

"Adrian Lazarus." He smiled as if this was the most natural meeting in the world. "You look well, considering. I see you've been drinking your shakes. Very good. How's school? Keeping your grades up, I hope."

"What are you doing here?"

"I work here," Dr. Halpert replied. "Kristoff and Kalvin are my employers, as well as my patients. My only patients, in fact. Besides you, of course, but you're special, aren't you?" he said, running his fingers down his thick mustache. "I head the research laboratory here at the compound."

"Really?" I said. "But I've been to your office. It was—"

He shook his head dismissively, "Oh, that was just for show. My real work is here. My research."

"What kind of research?"

"The best kind," Dr. Halpert said. He stepped closer to me, just a few feet away. "I seek a cure to man's gravest illness: death, of course."

I glanced up at the screen. "Are the brothers even

here? Or just images on TV? Why all this drama? The lights and the projections?"

Dr. Halpert gave an amused shrug. "The Borks are near, and very dangerous. Make no mistake about that, Adrian. But they are frail men, just the same. Not like you. No, not at all like you. Highly vulnerable to germs. It is my job to keep the brothers out of harm's way. As for the screen, what can I say? There's no business like business."

Up on the wall, the image of Kristoff Bork stared down on our conversation through small, dark, piercing eyes. Kalvin looked lost, incoherent, gravely unwell. I directed my question to Kristoff: "You are actually, seriously looking for a cure for death?"

Dr. Halpert answered, "Surely you realize that's why you've been brought here—to assist us with our research."

"Wait a minute," I said, sensing danger.

I became aware of a strange tingling in my fingers, unlike anything I had ever felt before. My knees buckled as I sensed another presence worming its way into my consciousness, as if a signal was attempting to reach me from a distant satellite. All I received was garbled static. I shook my head, slightly dazed, vaguely aware that Dr. Halpert seemed amused.

He grinned in a way I didn't like. The smile of a fox as it enters the henhouse. He tugged at his white lab coat, pulled on his whiskers. I'd seen that tic before.

Kristoff spoke up. "We are not unreasonable men, Adrian. We will pay handsomely for your services." There was eagerness in his voice, a minor note of desperation. He was trying to close the deal.

"The brothers do not have much time left," Dr. Halpert explained. "Surely you can see that. Kalvin, in particular, exists in a sort of twilight zone." He glanced up at the screen. "No, there's not much time left at all. Months, weeks, days."

Kristoff muttered, "Enough blather, Doctor. Let's finish this business. Nurse, bring my checkbook."

"And what if I refuse?" I said.

Kalvin fell into a spasm of coughing. His head flopped and lolled from side to side. Kristoff seemed to lean away from his brother, repulsed, a look of disgust on his face. Then his eyes returned to me, the way a sharpshooter zeroes in on a target.

"Have any idea what we do, boy? How we made our billions?" Kristoff didn't wait for my answer. "I'll tell you. We collect flashes of light, waves on computer screens, whispers in the dark corridors of the Internet—clicks, likes, comments, purchases, page views—in sum, we gather your digital footprint. But not only yours, Adrian. Don't think you are so special, boy."

I stiffened. "Don't call me boy."

Kristoff's lip curled. "Words, only words. But very well, Adrian. As you wish. We *own the data*. Like farmers, we reap what you sow. Then we sort and organize and sell in algorithms that are beyond your meager comprehension. In the end, we already own you—you've been bought and sold like a piece of meat."

"I'm free," I answered.

"Free? Oh, nonsense." Kristoff chuckled.

"You don't own me," I countered.

Kristoff smiled ruefully, as if conceding the

point. "We own only the digital footprint you so freely give away, Adrian. If you post a photo, we have a copy. If you send a text, we capture that, too, like a butterfly in our net."

"That's illegal. It's private," I said, surprised by my own anger.

"All your data points are known!" Kristoff's voice now rose in volume and venom. "To the world, you are only digital code, lines of ones and zeros signifying nothing. We've been where you've clicked, we've watched when you've blinked. We know what you buy, what you wear, and even what you secretly desire—often before you yourself are aware of it.

"There are no secrets from the data collectors."

I felt a whispery chill in my body. Like a great, cold hand had wrapped its fingers around me.

"You want to conduct experiments on me," I said. "That's it, isn't it? That's your research. You want to cut me up to help you live."

"I prefer the word *incision*," Dr. Halpert interjected. "*Cut up* seems so crude, like something out of *Frankenstein*." I'd almost forgotten he was standing there. "Think of it, Adrian. You may hold the secret to eternal life. The fountain of youth! If only we can get inside, unlock the mystery—"

"I have rights," I declared. "I don't care what you say. I won't be a subject for your experiments." I pointed a trembling finger at the wasted, shriveled brothers. "I'm not just another thing for you to use and throw away, like you've done to everything else on the planet. I refuse to be your guinea pig."

A fierce buzzing rippled through my mind as the volume of the white noise increased. And from that commotion of dizzying hiss, a single word slithered toward me like a snake across the carpet:

Escape, escape, escape.

I heard it clearly. I felt it clearly. Beyond speech, beyond ordinary language. It was a ripple of thought, a persistent hum. Something, or someone, was trying to send a message to me. My head pounded. *Escape*, it said. I felt a raw power surge through my body, an electric current of pure violence. I turned and moved quickly for the door, driven by animal instinct. The huge bodyguard stiffened to block my path.

I pointed back at the screen and demanded, "Let me leave!"

No answer.

I felt a surge of power inside me that was beyond myself. It was something other, and greater, than my ordinary being. My fingers curled, my muscles tightened. In that instant, I was not myself. The buzzing filled my head, louder and louder. My eyes locked on the vein in the bodyguard's neck. As I was about to attack, teeth bared, Kristoff's voice shouted out, "We have every intention of granting your request."

The guard rose from his defensive crouch. He looked, questioningly, toward Dr. Halpert.

"Let the boy go," the doctor instructed.

The big man stepped aside. His skin was ash white, as if he had just gazed into the visage of an avenging angel. I had scared him. I had scared the blood right out of his face.

I flung open the door, didn't look back.

Talal paced in the front courtyard. He stared

at me in wonder and, I think, with a shiver of apprehension. "It's all right," I angrily snapped. "Let's go. Now."

Once we got into the car and created some distance from the house, I slumped over, utterly exhausted. All energy drained out of me. As the limousine floated through the gathering darkness, over hills and into valleys, Talal ventured a question. "What happened in there?"

"I don't know," I admitted. "But I'm afraid." How could I explain that what I feared most . . . was my own self? The creature I was possibly becoming?

Talal didn't say a word. I could already detect the answer in his watchful eyes. He was afraid, too. We were silent the rest of way home.

When the car glided into town, I again heard the same high-pitched sound as before. I looked around for the source. An agitated bee probed the car window for an opening, gossamer wings batting against the glass. "Ah, there you are," Talal said. He pressed a button, the window soundlessly lowered, and the bee flew away.

THE HUNGER

I woke that night with a fierce, burning hunger. My mother's door was closed. I looked in on Dane, who still slept with a night-light, door ajar. I knelt beside his bed, listened to him breathe, his small chest rising and falling. He looked innocent sleeping there, a fragile creature.

He deserved a better world.

We all did.

I went downstairs, slipped on a sweatshirt, and stepped outdoors. I didn't think about what I was doing, didn't stop to ask myself where I was going.

I just walked, walked, walked—a zombie in the night—while hologram advertisements flashed across the sky.

The boy who'd come back from the dead, out for an evening stroll.

I felt lonely and afraid.

What had happened in that room with the Bork twins? I played the scene over in my mind. I had been ready to leap at that bodyguard's thick throat, clamp down on his jugular vein with my teeth, chomp on flesh and blood. All the while, I didn't feel like I was in control. It was as if I was following some deeper instinct for survival.

I pushed aside thoughts of the Bork brothers. For now, at least, I didn't want to worry about them. I just wanted to be me, whoever that was.

I noticed that my limp had gone away. I was walking normally now. There was even a bounce in my step. I felt like I could jump, I could run a mile. I could hop on a pogo stick and bounce, bounce, bounce. What was happening to me? Why had I become this strange shifting creature?

I remembered something I'd learned from

Zander. He must have read it somewhere. Two years ago, a group of scientists announced to the world that a star had disappeared. Not just any star, but the North Star, Polaris, the guiding light by which sailors for ages had determined east and west, north and south. The bright star had held nearly still at the celestial pole, marking due north. Then one day, whoops, it vanished. Not into thin air, but into thinner nothingness. Nobody had ever seen anything like it. Sure, stars die. Stars burn out and explode into supernovas. Stars shed their outer layers, transform into white dwarfs, black dwarfs. Stars burn hydrogen for billions of years, then take millions of years to die. Not our North Star. It just disappeared without a trace. Basically, the best scientists in the world scratched their beards, adjusted their glasses, scanned the data, and concluded, "Weird."

No wonder we'd lost our way.

I paused, looked around. I'd come to a wooded area behind a small apartment complex. There was a gully with a small stream. I sniffed the air, nostrils flaring. My sense of smell was returning, better than ever. A new, worrying thing.

Meat and blood.

I smelled a fresh kill.

And there, down by the water's edge, I spied a fox with a rabbit in its bloody mouth. The fox's ears twitched and it froze, eyes locked on me.

Snap, a twig broke beneath my foot. My approach spooked the quick brown fox; it dropped the dead rabbit and darted safely away into the underbrush. For a horrifying moment, I felt an urge, like a tidal tug, to get down into the muck on my hands and knees to feast on the fresh kill.

I waited for the feeling to pass.

That wasn't me. I might have been undead, but I refused to cross that line again.

I sat beside the stream, gazing at my shadowy reflection in the rippled, starlit water. Somehow from that perspective, a new thought entered my consciousness as clearly as if I were reading the words in a book. It was such a new thought—a 180-degree turnaround—that it took me a moment to fully accept the truth of it.

I was a zombie.

But I still had control. I was responsible for my own actions.

I wasn't a coal-burning factory spewing toxic waste into the sky. I wasn't an oil spill, a raging fire, a standardized test, an airborne disease, a science-denying politician, or a big-time businessman willing to destroy the planet just because our government had failed to protect us.

I wasn't the problem with this world.

But I might be part of the solution.

In that sense, at least, I guess I was just like everybody else.

SETTING THE TRAP

On Friday, the day of the "Halloween Fandango"—don't look at me, I don't name these things—Principal Rouster made another major announcement:

Kkkccchh. Kkkccchh. Tap-tap. TAP-TAP—SQUAAAWWWKKK. "Good afternoon, Nixon Middle School! Due to the recent discovery of toxic mold in various locations around the school, the Department of Health has temporarily shut down gymnasium B, our proposed setting for tonight's Halloween Fandango!"

My classmates wore mixed expressions: a

contrast of (1) disappointed or (2) intensely relieved. Principal Rouster, however, had more to say. "Not to worry! We've moved the dance to . . . THE PIT!"

Churlish screams, anguished cries, and wails of despair filled the room. "Not the pit, anything but the pit!" Desiree Reynolds moaned.

"It smells like stale cheese!" groaned Arnie Chang.

"I got sick in the pit last year," little Jessica Timmons confessed in her tiny voice, "and they still haven't mopped it up."

What's the pit? If you imagine our ancient, half-condemned middle school building as a concrete giant, then the pit would be, well, the armpit: a cramped, damp, dank, and low-ceilinged basement, smelling vaguely of mustard, sweat, and old tacos. In other words, great if you are a mushroom, not terrific for a middle school dance.

I didn't really care. Under normal circumstances, I would have skipped the dance altogether, except for Zander's elaborate plot to finally gain the upper hand on Daryl Northrop. "We can't let him bully us any longer," Zander had decided. The plan was a simple con. We hoped to convince Daryl, for a little while at least, that I was honestly and truly a dangerous zombie, capable of hideous acts of violence and gastronomy.

It was an acting job, basically, with a cast of dozens. We planned to put on a performance, complete with special effects. Zander had recruited his cousin Clare, the makeup artist, and she had gladly embraced the challenge. She and some of her theater friends were set to meet me at an appointed hour in the woods behind school.

First, we had to survive the dance.

A crowd of girls moved and bounced on the dance floor, smiling and laughing to the music, perfectly happy. A few boys joined them, but not many. Over by the snack table, a lumpy knot of guys stood around, tugging at their ties, watching the girls. I found Zander, clutching a cupcake as if his life depended on it. "We're all set?" I asked.

"Be ready," he said, and walked away.

I leaned against the wall and took in the scene. The room was too dark, too loud, too crowded—and everyone seemed almost desperate in their attempt to have "the best time ever." A sadness descended upon me like a heavy fog, a blanket of doubt. I didn't belong there, and I acutely felt my separateness; my unlife was all a horrible mistake, somebody's idea of a celestial practical joke. Hand over my heart, I felt nothing—not a beat, not a liquid thrum, not the faintest fillip. Gia once called me a survivor, and that was true. But I didn't understand why. Curious, I had looked up *zombie* in the dictionary. It read: "a soulless corpse said to have been revived by witchcraft." This was another definition: "a dull, apathetic, or slow-witted person." There's also the description, *zombielike,* meaning "characteristic of or resembling a zombie; lifeless, unfeeling."

And there it was, that word: *unfeeling.* How that one word pained me. I felt, I cared, I hurt. I was a person just like everybody else, and yet it didn't seem like that at all. Across the room I glimpsed

Daryl Northrup, sneering and chewing gum open-mouthed, watching the girls dance. Talal threaded his way through the crowd toward Daryl.

"If looks could kill," Gia commented. She handed me a cup of red juice. "You okay?"

"Just great," I murmured. "Do you really think this plan will work?"

"I know it will," Gia answered.

"How do you know?" I asked.

"I just . . . do," she shrugged. "You haven't said how nice I look."

I leaned away, surprised. Gia stared down at me—she was quite a bit taller—through calm, wide-set eyes. She wore a sleeveless black dress that stopped two inches above her knees, a thin belt clasped at her narrow hips. Her purple hair seemed to glow as if lit from within. "You look . . . amazing," I admitted.

Gia took my tie playfully between her fingers. "Fancy," she said.

"My mother found it in a closet," I said.

"Ah," Gia said. We saw Talal, who stood in ready position near Daryl's elbow.

It was almost time.

"You look good," she told me.

"Don't sound so surprised," I chided her.

"No, seriously. Your face, your skin. Something has changed." She searched my eyes for an answer.

I shrugged. "Shakes, I guess."

"I guess," Gia said, but not like she believed me. Right on time, she placed her hand on my chest, directly above my silent heart. If it was part of the act, it was worth an Oscar. Something stirred inside me.

At that moment, Zander charged over, grabbed Gia by the wrist, and yanked her toward the dance floor. "Get away from him," he demanded, loudly enough for everyone to hear.

It had begun.

"Hey!" I shouted.

Gia gazed at me for a split second with an expression of loss, as if a cord had been cut, and she twirled away, dancing in Zander's arms. They moved across the floor, spinning and whirling.

"Not too close," snapped a chaperone.

I saw their hips move in rhythm. Funny, for a

"supersize me" type of guy, Zander looked surprisingly smooth on the dance floor. Gia smiled, put her head on his shoulder. Across the room, a million miles away, she looked at me and nodded.

Now.

I pushed my way through the churning dance floor, barking accusations. "What are you doing with her?" I said. "I thought you were my friend!"

Zander turned his back to me, still holding Gia tight. "Get a life," he said over his shoulder.

I reached for Gia's wrist. Zander slapped my hand away. Eyes narrowed, mouth tight, he spit: "I said: Get a life, freak."

He again turned his back to me, so I grabbed Zander by the shoulder, spun him around, and landed a right cross to his face. Zander fell backward, spilling Daryl Northrup's drink in the process.

"Fight!" Talal cried.

"Fight!" another voice called out.

The crowd jostled and pressed closer for a better view.

"Out!" a chaperone demanded. In a moment,

Principal Rouster pushed me up the stairs and toward the exit. "This isn't over!" I screamed over my shoulder. "Tonight, ten o'clock, Zander, by the log in the woods!"

Moments later, the school door slammed behind me. I found myself outside in a parking lot. Now it was up to Talal to do his work, whispering in Daryl's ear. I hurried across the field, up the hill, and into the woods.

Things were going according to plan.

A REAL, FLESH-EATING ZOMBIE

I found Clare waiting by the dirt clearing with several other people I didn't know. This was a location long established by neighborhood teenagers, the ground strewn with candy wrappers and abandoned beer bottles from years of weekend gatherings. It was an ugly sight. I promised myself that we'd return another day to clean it up.

"Right on time," Clare said, stepping forward to

greet me. "How did it go in there? Did you pull it off?"

"I hope so," I said, rubbing the knuckles of my right hand. "I punched your cousin pretty hard."

"It had to look real," Clare said, absolving me of guilt. "Come, let me show you the props."

We went over the routine again. Clare introduced me to the others, friends from her improvisational theater club at school. They wore colorful outfits and complicated haircuts. To them, tonight was just another show, a fun piece of performance art for Halloween, a zombie play with blood and gore. Clare picked up a heavy tree branch that rested against the trunk of an oak. "The fight has to look convincing," she said. "So you've got to really bring it down hard when you hit Zander across the back."

"You sure it won't hurt him?"

"Don't worry about Zander, he's wearing extra padding. And look," Clare said. She ran a finger across a thin crack that ran midway across the stick. "It's already broken, pieced together with clear packing tape." Clare stepped back and waved the stick through the air like a Jedi knight. "It should hold together when you swing it, but the stick will snap easily when it comes down on his back." She carefully laid it on the ground.

"What about the intestines?" I asked.

A boy stepped forward. His skin was a shade lighter than mine. "I'm Ahmed," he said, shaking my hand. He explained that his father was the butcher in town and that he had "liberated" a long strand of uncut sausage links. "The problem is the meat's not cooked, so you'll have to fake eating it."

I nodded. Raw meat would not be a problem.

Ahmed turned to Clare, gestured to the half-dozen teenagers gathered around. "The sky is overcast, so it's plenty dark, and we'll make sure your target doesn't get too close a view."

"Remember, it's got to be chaotic and loud," Clare told the group.

A garble of voices filtered up from below. "Here they come," someone said.

"All right, we'll disappear into the woods for now," Clare said. She winked at me. "Break a leg, Adrian."

Down below, a small mob of students crossed

the field in a dark blob. Spotlights from the school building threw long shadows across the grass as the bubbling, burbling mass drew near. I could make out Zander in the lead, hand still held to his cheek. His long strides were purposeful, like he was eager for a fight. Talal walked close to Daryl, yammering in his ear, surely urging him to come see the great entertainment: Zander Donnelly versus Adrian Lazarus, fighting over a girl—may they both beat each other senseless! Dozens of students tagged along, many of them in on the deceit. That had been Gia's job, to let everybody know we were pranking Daryl, who surely deserved it.

Our little play worked to perfection. Zander charged forward, tackling me to the ground. We tussled and rolled around in the dirt and leaves. The crowd gathered around, with Clare's friends stepping forward, half blocking Daryl's view. Zander gained the advantage and viciously kicked me in the stomach while I was still on the ground. I didn't feel a thing; zombies never do.

"Kill 'im, kill 'im!" I heard Daryl scream.

My hand found the stick. I rose, swung it menacingly in the air, and smashed Clare's prop down on Zander's back. Zander cried out in pain, staggered for a moment, and fell into a thicket. A stunned hush fell over the gathered throng. I gave a guttural groan like a feral beast. Before anyone could move, I leaped beside Zander's fallen body, making sure to keep my back to Daryl. I burst a large packet of fake blood that had been planted inside Zander's shirt. While Zander shrieked in agony, my two hands tore up the string of sausages that had been hidden in a hollow. They dripped with bloody sauce.

"Oh my God, that's his intestines!" Clare cried, followed by bloodcurdling screams.

"He's a cannibal!" another person howled.

I spun around in the dirt, crawling like Gollum from *Lord of the Rings*. Daryl and the others backed away, staring in horror. I moaned hungrily, pointed a crooked finger at Daryl. "You're next," I threatened. My teeth violently tore into a fistful of sausages; I groaned with animal pleasure at the taste of delicious blood (watered-down marinara sauce!) that gushed from my mouth.

"He's gone crazy!" Gia shrieked.

"Run! Go! Go!" other voices screamed.

The crowd, on cue, imploded into chaos. Someone, somewhere, lit off a packet of firecrackers. A smoke bomb went off. Students fled in blind terror. From behind, Ahmed knocked Daryl to the ground. Daryl scrambled desperately in the dirt. Tears streaming from his eyes, he called out, "Help me, Mama! Help me!"

He got to his feet—I lunged forward, arms outstretched, clawing at his shirt—and Daryl ran screaming out of the woods and into the night.

I almost felt sorry for him.

But not quite.

For a long instant, we held our breath and watched Daryl flee. Finally, the coast clear, I hugged Gia, clasped an arm around Zander's shoulders. Talal joined our celebratory group, depositing a cell phone into his coat pocket. "That was awesome!" he screamed into the night.

Clare congratulated Zander, then me. "You guys

deserve an Academy Award. That was fantastic! Hysterical! Brilliant!"

"Thanks to your help," I replied.

A frown crossed Clare's face. She appeared troubled. "But . . . if you don't mind my saying so . . . I don't see what you guys accomplished tonight. The next time Daryl sees Zander, he's going to realize that he was tricked. He'll get angry, maybe even dangerous."

"That's why I texted him a link to the video I just filmed," Talal said.

"You got it on camera?" Clare asked.

Talal smiled. "Oh yes, I sure did—and it's very entertaining. Four stars, easy."

We roared with laughter, once again congratulating Zander for a brilliant plan.

Finger flicking, Talal scrolled through his cell. "I included a note. Here, let me read it:

"'Dear Daryl, don't stress, Zander's fine. You got punked, bigly. Before you get angry, please take a moment to view the short video attached. Pretty embarrassing, don't you think? We promise not to share this video . . . it will be our little secret . . . as long as you never bother anyone at school ever again. If you do, we'll download the video for all the world to see. We think it could go viral. Yes, this is called BLACKMAIL.

"'Sincerely, Adrian Lazarus, Talal Mirwani, Gia Demeter, and Zander Donnelly.'"

TALAL PAYS A VISIT

I awoke the next morning feeling refreshed. Alive, almost. Ready to go. When I rose, I clapped my hands and did a little shuffle. Here was something to celebrate. A new me, a whole new way of looking at things. The next question was simple yet troubling: How does a seventh grader go about fixing the world? I replayed the previous night's triumph over Daryl and chuckled to myself. The answer was obvious: We'll have to save the world one creep at a time.

Still dead, but cautiously optimistic, I considered the day ahead. It was Halloween. I had promised to dress as the Tin Man and take Dane trick-or-treating. Zander would be the Cowardly Lion. Gia had agreed to dress as Dorothy in red shoes and a blue gingham dress. Together, we'd follow the Yellow Brick Road to Candyland.

When I went downstairs, I glanced out the window and saw Talal kicking a soccer ball with Dane. Unnoticed, I paused to admire them at play. Talal tossed aside his trench coat and dazzled Dane with his nimble moves. Dane squealed and fell to the ground, laughing.

I stepped onto the front stoop. "Who's winning?"

Dane leaped up and ran to me. "Your friend is here again! He's really good at soccer!"

Talal rolled the ball in our direction. I shook my head. "I don't think so."

"Try, Adrian," Dane encouraged me. "It's fun."

I gave the ball a soft tap with the side of my formerly floppy foot. It held firm. Dane darted forward, gave the ball a mighty boot across the yard, and flew after it. Dane was funny when he ran, the faces he made, as if squinching his eyes tightly made him go faster.

"That kid cracks me up," Talal said, gathering up his coat.

"What are you doing here?" I asked.

"We should talk," he said. "We haven't since, you know, that night."

I knew that he was right. I couldn't ignore the Borks any longer.

I shouted to Dane, "Hey! Don't cross the street!"

Dane stood at the edge of the grass. He looked longingly at his ball, which had bounded across the road to a neighbor's lawn. He called back, "Now can I?"

"Did you look both ways?"

Dane made an exaggerated show of looking down the road in each direction, hand flat above his brow like a sailor in the crow's nest. There wasn't a car in sight.

"Go," I said.

Dane went like a miniature lightning bolt. He fell on the ball with an outrageous tumble, scooped it up, and ran back again.

"Let's play!" he said, kicking the ball to me.

"I can't."

"Please!"

"Not now. But later, I promise," I said.

"Pinkie swear!"

I laughed—"Get outta here, twerp"—and kicked the ball a mile. Not bad.

Talal and I went around back to sit under the patio umbrella—safe, we hoped, from prying eyes. "So?" I asked.

"Remember all that building equipment we saw up at the Bork estate?" Talal asked. "I got curious about it, so I did a little research."

"You went back up there?"

"No, I reprogrammed the drone that we knocked out of the sky." Talal smiled, pleased with himself. "I think that's called irony, right? Using one of the Borks' own drones to spy on them. Or maybe it's poetic justice, I'm not sure."

"Either way, nicely done," I complimented him. "What did you find out?"

"I think they're building . . . some kind of medical

facility," he said. "They have huge crates of operating equipment, all kinds of expensive machinery."

It confirmed what Dr. Halpert had told me.

Talal took off his hat, turned it round and round in his hands. "I know, it's bizarre," he said. "The structure went up really quickly, definitely not part of the main house. It's a separate building entirely. The walls are lined with lead. Whatever they've got planned for that building, they want to keep it a secret."

I needed a drink. "Water?" I offered.

"You got anything stronger?"

"Grape juice?"

Talal nodded. "Make it a tall one."

I returned with two filled glasses and a bowl of chips, which neither of us touched.

"I haven't told you everything that happened that day," I said.

Talal looked up. And like always, he waited, as a good detective should.

I filled the silence. "The medical facility makes sense. They want to conduct experiments."

"On you?"

"Yeah, on me," I said. "The Borks are dying. Or at least one of them looks like toast already. They seem to think that I might be the cure."

Talal held the juice glass between his hands meditatively.

I recalled the buzzing I'd sensed when I was in the room with the Borks. The garbled static that had filled my head. The word that had threaded its way to me: *escape, escape, escape.*

For some reason, I didn't tell Talal about the buzzing. Perhaps he already knew. There had been that stray bee in the limo during the ride home. What had Tal said? *Ah, there you are.*

The gumshoe downed his juice with one gulp. "Riddle me this, Adrian: Do you really think it's over? That the mighty Borks of K & K are going to let you just waltz out of there? Two of the most powerful men in the world, defeated by a zombie boy?"

"I didn't defeat them," I said.

"That's what worries me," Tal replied. "They don't seem to be the type to take 'no' for an answer."

I told him he was probably right. Then I remembered: "There was a nurse in the room with them."

"Are you sure?"

"Yes, I saw her in the hallway. Later on, Kristoff said, 'Nurse, bring my checkbook.'"

"That confirms it," Talal said, clapping his hands together. "It wasn't some trick with technology. The Borks are really there in the building. Maybe in the next room!"

"Well, that's good, I guess," I said. "At least I wasn't talking to a phony image on a television screen."

"Be careful," Talal warned. "I'll keep working the drone, talking with my hacker friends. Let's see if I can come up with any answers."

"Thanks, Tal. I don't know where I'd be without your help."

"I'm just a gumshoe," he said, adjusting his hat as he stood. "Gia's the one who hired me. You should thank her."

Gia, I thought.

The girl who'd been stung by a thousand bees.

I wondered how she'd liked the limo.

THEN, SUDDENLY, GONE

There was no point trick-or-treating before dusk, so we took it slow that afternoon. My mom hung around all day, decorating the house with pumpkins and wicked witches, busting moves to old Motown sounds, and helping us with our costumes. She even pulled out a battered sewing machine, something I hadn't seen her do in years. Together we made buffalo chicken dip—which I nibbled out of politeness—and watched a game on ESPN47. It was all so average. Out of nowhere she said, "This is nice, being together."

She squeezed my hand.

I thought it was nice, too, so I grunted back. In the back of my mind, I kept mulling over that morning's conversation with Talal. Why hadn't the Borks come after me already? And if they did, how could I protect myself?

Dane was ready and fully costumed by five o'clock, loose bits of straw drifting to the floor. Super excited, he pestered me to act out with him the scene from the movie when Dorothy first meets the Scarecrow. Dane had every word and gesture committed to memory. "You have to ask which way," he demanded.

"Okay, as long as you don't make me get off the couch," I said, lazily stuffing another chip in my mouth. In a poor imitation of Dorothy, I asked in a high voice, "Now which way do we go, Toto?"

Dane pointed left, arm fully extended, and said in his best Scarecrow voice, "Pardon me, that way is a very nice way." After a pause, he switched arms and said, "It's pleasant down that way, too!"

"Too bad we don't have a dog to play Toto," I commented.

Dane refused to break character. Scarecrow continued, "Of course, people do go both ways!"

He shook his head no, nodded yes, and pointed in both directions simultaneously. Scarecrow went on to explain, quite thoughtfully, that he didn't have a brain.

I was saved from another hour of acting out scenes from the movie when the doorbell rang. It was Zander and Gia—already dressed for Halloween. Zander looked decent as the Cowardly Lion. The tail was right, anyway. But Gia was stunning with her hair parted in the middle, tied in blue bows that matched her blue-checkered dress. She even carried an old-fashioned handbasket.

"There's no place like home," Gia said, entering our living room.

Dane stood awestruck. "Dorothy," he murmured.

Gia curtsied, bending her knees and bowing graciously. "And you must be Scarecrow," she said. "I'm pleased to meet you."

My costume required silver face paint, about a thousand feet of aluminum foil, and a silver funnel hat that was strapped to my chin. My mother touched up Zander's face paint, and after a few photographs, it was time to go. She called to me from the front door. "Keep a close eye on your brother, and don't eat too much junk!"

We led Dane to the more expensive neighborhoods, where most trick-or-treaters clustered. Better candy in large amounts, as simple as that. Gia, Zander, and I all felt a little corny in our Oz costumes—we were borderline too old for Halloween—but Dane's electric, over-the-moon presence made everything okay. He sang and danced and twirled around, swinging his ever-bulging pillowcase in the air. *If I only had a brain!* As the night deepened, the costumes on our fellow trick-or-treaters gradually shifted from Pixar movie characters to edgier costumes worn by older kids. The usual stuff: chain-saw killers, nuclear mutants, and, of course, werewolves and zombies.

Lots of zombies.

I tried not to let it bother me. But think about it: How would you like it if people dressed up as *you* for Halloween? Like it's a great big joke, be a zombie for a night, then wash off the gunk before climbing between cool white bedsheets. *Ha-ha-ha.* I'd like to see them try it with lung tissues liquefying and a pancreas in shreds. What if I dressed up exactly like everybody else: the jeans, the football jersey, the new kicks, and the same twenty-dollar haircut. What do they do, sit in the barber's chair and say, *Give me the same cut as everybody else*?

I don't think I wanted that, either.

Rats. A zombie heart might not beat, but it can still ache.

After a while, we stopped going door-to-door with Dane, who was super hyped up on candy. He ran up and down the walkways and across the lawns: giddy and joyful, cute as a puppy.

The sidewalks were filled with ever-changing groups of trick-or-treaters. I spied one figure in a yellow beekeeper's outfit, head veiled. He or she never got close but seemed to be around every corner, lurking behind every tree.

"Hi, Cheryl," Gia greeted a girl dressed as a cheerleader with an ax in her head.

"Who's that?" I asked.

"Cheryl," Zander dryly stated.

"Beyond the name," I said.

"Just a girl," Gia replied. "Why, do you think she's pretty?"

I laughed. "Call me picky, but I'm not really into girls with axes stuck in their heads."

Gia said "hmmmph" and walked ahead.

She almost seemed jealous. Could it be possible? Zander poked me on the shoulder. "You guys see Dane?"

"He's around here somewhere." I swiveled my head. Up the street. Down the street. I checked the doors to the houses for stray trick-or-treaters. The neighborhood had nearly emptied. "Dane?" I called. "Dane!"

Gia and Zander picked up the cry. We walked, and then ran, up and down the street. "Dane! DANE!"

"Stay calm," Zander advised. "Dane probably got swept up with another group in the excitement. We'll split up and—"

A long black limousine pulled up. The passenger-side window slid down. There he was, smiling back at us.

"Dane!" I exclaimed.

"Get in, all of you," the driver ordered. His face was half hidden in shadow, but it was one I would never forget—the burly, unsmiling bodyguard from the Borks' estate. The guy I nearly ate.

I snatched for the door handle. "Run, Dane!" I shouted.

Click. The automatic lock snapped down, the window rolled halfway up. Through the window, I watched as the driver leaned closer to my brother. He put a gloved hand on Dane's shoulder.

It was the simplest of gestures. Even gentle, in some ways. But the threat was unmistakable.

"Get in, Adrian," the man repeated.

Desperate, I looked around. The street was empty except for the lone beekeeper, moving away from us, sliding seamlessly into the shadows.

We had no choice.

We climbed into the car.

Dr. Halpert was waiting in the backseat, a relaxed smile on his face. "Has anyone got any chocolate they'd care to share?"

A SECRET REVEALED

The cell vibrated in my back pocket. I slyly checked it, hoping to hide it from Dr. Halpert. I assumed it would be from my mother, but I didn't recognize the number. The message box was empty except for a lone ampersand, like a signal from a ghost.

Or a message from someone too cautious to speak.

I thought of the beekeeper, dressed in yellow,

that I'd seen lurking in the shadows. I punched in one word: *Gumshoe?*

Y came the reply.

Dr. Halpert held out his hand. "I'll take your phone."

I hesitated.

"My mother," I said. "She wants me to keep in touch."

He showed me his clean, tidy white teeth. "This is unpleasant business, Adrian. A sorry turn of events. It's up to you what happens tonight. Just cooperate with us, and in a few hours you'll be home, snug as a bug in bed."

"What about my brother?"

"Dane will be unharmed, of course," the doctor reassured. "We are not monsters, Adrian. Look at him in the front seat, happily eating candy and watching cartoons. He thinks this is fun. Your brother was merely a device for getting you into the car."

Merely a device. The phrase echoed in my head.

Gia sat across from me, arms crossed, scowling.

I said, "I would have come without all the drama."

Dr. Halpert slipped our phones into the pocket of his suit jacket. My lifeline to Talal, buried in a blue blazer with brass buttons. "Kristoff has a particular vision for you," the doctor said in soothing tones. "It was imperative that we prevented you from notifying others. No one can know where you are tonight. The Borks did not wish for any . . . untoward interruptions."

Zander and Gia sat glaring at Halpert, their backs to the driver. The car was so spacious we could have stretched out our legs without touching. Neither spoke, but Gia's eyes were active and alert. I could almost hear the wheels in her mind furiously spinning. Zander looked at me through moist eyes, and I could see that he was afraid. He nervously tore through a package of Twizzlers.

Talal, at least, knew where we were headed. I hoped he could help us. We drove the rest of the way in silence, broken only by the sound of Dane's laughter in the front seat. A mouse was beating a cat over the head with a giant hammer. The kid thought it was hysterical.

Back in the vast lobby of the estate, I paused to

shed what was left of my costume. It had started
to fall apart five minutes after I put it on in the
first place. A round K & K logo hung between in-
dividual portraits of the brothers, each in his own
golden frame. I hadn't studied the paintings my
first time through the estate. The paintings gave a
puzzling effect. Each portrait was a head shot, tightly
focused on the brother's face. I couldn't put my finger on it, but something about the paintings seemed
unnatural.

As a group, we walked down the same hallways
I'd walked before. Dr. Halpert, smooth and ever
smiling, led the way. I held Dane's hand, sticky
from Skittles, while Gia and Zander came next. The
thuggish guard took up the rear, his face impassive
as always. I stopped to tie my shoe, lagging behind,
furtively glancing around for some kind of clue.
Where's the nurse? I wondered.

"Come along, this way," Dr. Halpert chirped with
birdlike insistence. The large bodyguard placed a
thick hand on my back and shoved me forward.

Gia caught me, leaned in close to my ear. "Got
you," she whispered.

"You do?"

Dr. Halpert stamped his heel sharply on the parquet floor. "Really, I must insist, no more delays!" He recovered to flash a false smile at Dane, then pivoted his gaze to me. The smile disappeared. We stood outside the same door I had entered a few days ago. His hand reached for the knob.

"I'll cooperate," I said. "But I want to see them first."

Dr. Halpert's head tilted, unsure of what I was asking.

"Not in this room, not on TV." I gestured to the door farther up the hallway. Where I had seen the nurse on my last visit. "In that room. Face-to-face. Or no deal."

The doctor's eyes narrowed. He stood fully erect, shoulders pulled back. And once again, his fingers stroked the sides of his thick mustache.

"Very well, I will see what my employers think of your proposal," he purred. "Wait here. And do not move, do not try to leave." He nodded at the guard, who instantly squeezed his meaty fingers around Gia's and Zander's arms.

Moments later, we entered the darkened inner chamber of the legendary Bork brothers. Faint light fell from a chandelier without quite reaching the carpeted floor. The twins were propped up by pillows on a wide bed, and they watched without emotion as we entered. Heavy blankets were pulled high, nearly to their chins. Their heads, I saw, seemed in unnaturally close proximity. Their necks were twisted like old tree limbs, as if it pained them to look forward.

Two brothers in the same bed?

That close together?

"Step forward, Adrian," Kristoff said. This was his true voice. Thin and brittle.

Gia, Zander, and Dane huddled behind me.

"They only want me," I assured them. "It's all right. We'll go home soon. Together."

I moved to the edge the bed. Tubes and wires ran from under the blankets to a station of complex medical equipment, computers, and flashing screens. The young nurse sat in a nearby chair, hands delicately folded on her lap. She had red lips, blond hair, and the pale, slender neck of a white swan. Today she wore lemon-colored surgical scrubs.

Kristoff spoke. "Forgive the darkness. As you can see, we are frail old men, sensitive to the light, like fine wine stored in musty cellars."

His voice crackled. He paused to take shallow breaths after every few words, as if it took a strenuous effort merely to speak a sentence.

The other brother, Kalvin, peered at me through sunken pink eyes. He coughed a wet, phlegmy death rattle, and both men winced at once. Kalvin's head rolled from side to side as if he were about to fall asleep.

"Do you not yet understand?" Kristoff asked. "Doctor, the blanket, if you please."

Dr. Halpert bent forward and gently, slowly folded the blanket down to the waist, revealing the secret that the Borks had kept hidden from the world all these years. They were joined at the torso. They shared one chest and wore baby-blue silk pajamas. I shivered. The air felt exceptionally cold, as if the conjoined twins had been kept refrigerated, like rare orchids at a florist's shop. It struck me that

Kristoff and Kalvin had likely been attached to machines all their lives, necks unnaturally twisted so they wouldn't have to stare continuously into the other's face. It was hard to tell exactly where the machines ended and the men began.

WHEN IT RAINS

"A pretty picture, are we not?" Kristoff said in a thin, weak voice. He chuckled softly. "So now, at last, you see our predicament."

I moved to the very edge of the bed, where the twins lay. Kalvin seemed even sicker in real life, his weary head now sunken into the soft pillow, eyes open but vacant, a string of spittle dribbling from his mouth. A battery of machines beeped and whirred against the wall. There was a silver oxygen tank beside the bed.

"This time we meet under less pleasant circumstances," Kristoff hissed, lingering, snakelike, on each S sound. "You have not been cooperative."

Exhausted from the effort, he let his head fall back against the pillow. The nurse moved to adjust the liquid dripping into the IV tube that ran into his arm.

She then stepped to the far side of the bed and brought a small penlight to Kalvin's eyes. The old man stared blankly, stupefied, unseeing. She bent close and frowned.

Kristoff raised his head to stare at me, momentarily revived.

I stood in the deep gloom of a room filled with sickness, and sensed the nearness of death, as if it were another creature in the bed beside them. "What do you want with me?" I asked.

Kristoff smirked, eyes closed. "Life. What else is there?"

I said, "I don't understand. Why me?"

"My dear brother is rapidly failing. We believe that you hold the key to my—to *our*—freedom,"

Kristoff said. He slithered out a bony hand from beneath the covers. His fingers were arthritic, gnarled into mangled shapes. Kristoff reached the trembling claw toward me, shaking from the effort. "You will give us the secret, boy Lazarus."

He fell back in a fit of coughing. For all his wealth, he was just a twisted, broken old man, his body racked with disease. Dr. Halpert produced a large syringe from a black leather bag. He held it up, frowned at the weak light cast by the chandelier, flicked the needle once, and plunged it deep into the shared chest of the twins. He went around to the other side of the bed, checking on Kalvin, touching his neck, gazing into his eyes. The doctor shook his head. "We're running out of time."

The nurse brought the oxygen mask to Kristoff's face. His eyes closed to a reptilian slit as the machine-forced air filled his lungs. After a moment, his eyes snapped open. He lifted his hand, signaling for the nurse to sit.

Kristoff's eyes widened. Revived by the shot, his head coiled upward, cobra-like. This time he spoke with more strength. "Yes, time is of the essence."

"It should be an almost painless process, considering your damaged nervous system," Dr. Halpert informed me, as if something had just been decided. "I am skilled in the art of the knife. I simply need to take small samples, run tests, poke around."

I looked back to see Zander, Gia, and Dane clustered in a tight knot. Gia had bent to her knees with both arms protectively around Dane. She was whispering to him, touching his hair and face, working to keep him calm. As my eyes roamed the room, I noticed that the long burgundy drapes that covered the windows had been parted slightly. I could see a few faint stars in the sky, pale flecks of light that had traveled like arrows for thousands of years through blackest space to shine precisely now outside the window. Everything dies: stars, planets, galaxies. Even the Milky Way will one day whirl into a black hole. Yet in that instant, I glimpsed a movement, a faint shape, a hope hovering outside the window.

Not a bird, but a drone.

Talal was watching. I knew it in my bones.

I looked away, not wishing to draw attention to Talal's drone.

"Come, we are wasting time, Doctor," Kristoff snapped. Spittle flew from his mouth.

"Wait, I have an offer!" I announced, stalling for time. "If you want me to help save your lives, I want you to change your ways. Promise that you'll use your money to help protect the environment."

The doctor snickered but made no move. He waited for Kristoff's reply.

"After all," I continued, "you've dedicated your lives to destroying it. You drill in the Arctic, you dump waste in our rivers, pump cancer-causing chemicals into the earth. You pollute the atmosphere, you stop at nothing—"

"Silence!" Kristoff ordered, flicking his tongue past thin lips. "The time for negotiation has passed."

"Even now in your misery," I said, "you only care about one thing: more, more, more. When will it be enough?"

A smile crossed Kristoff's face, a snake slinking across a barren desert wasteland. He was amused by me.

I asked, in a soft voice, "What's the point of living forever if our planet is ruined in the process? Look at this world that people like you have left us—floods and fires, earthquakes and droughts, rain forests cut down, entire species wiped off the planet, toxic water—"

"And you blame us for this? We, the great men of industry and progress?" Kristoff asked, head trembling. "We are the job creators! You foolish, idealistic child. You little boy. You lollipop, you dum-dum. You know nothing about the world. Nothing about how it really works."

"I know what's right," I said.

"You know *nothing*!" he spit out.

"I'll never help you—I hope you both die!"

"That's enough," Dr. Halpert stated

Kristoff lifted the oxygen mask to his face and breathed deeply from it. Kalvin coughed weakly, eyes wandering, unfocused. The machines beeped and whirred in the background. The nurse began to stir again, uncrossing her legs, but Kristoff waved her off with a peevish flick of the hand.

"No, no, no," the old man protested. "I find the

boy spirited and entertaining. Let him prattle."
Kristoff muffled a cough in his curled hand.

But I had already said all that I had to say. I
stood facing them, sapped of strength.

Kristoff purred, cold eyes gleaming. "And after
we die, Adrian? What then?" His eyes slid to the
machines at his right. "We are only part of a greater
engine. After we go, the machine marches on.
K & K will continue, and it will do what it does
best—it earns profits. That's what corporations do.
K & K will make money, filling someone else's
pockets with gold while people like you fill their
heads with fear and needless worry."

He gave a long and hollow laugh, flashing yel-
lowed, decayed teeth. He spit into his pillow. Red
dots of blood appeared on it. Death was not far away.

"You have no answers," Kristoff said. "What
could you possibly know, a boy your age? What
comes after us? You see, our advantage over you is
simply this: We do not care."

He grinned wickedly, delighted with his own
words.

"We don't care what comes next. That's your

weakness, Adrian. You fret too much. Why not follow our example? Get rich. Be happy."

Dr. Halpert yanked me by the arm. The bodyguard came forward to grab my other wrist, twisting it high behind my back. The contortion didn't hurt, but I was trapped all the same. The time for talk had ended. I swiveled my head to look out the window. "Now!" I cried, desperately hoping that Talal and his hacker friends could hear me.

"Now, now, now!"

Instantly, fire alarms blared.

Lights flashed like dizzying strobes, pulsing in the dark.

Torrents of water poured from the ceiling sprinklers.

FIRE

"The sprinklers!" bellowed Dr. Halpert in exasperation. Popping sounds came from the machines; sparks flew, systems short-circuited. The Borks lay in the bed, helplessly soaked, with Kristoff muttering curses.

I watched as a joyous smile came to Kalvin's face, like that of an innocent child exalting in an afternoon sun shower.

Then chaos erupted.

It took a moment for me to realize that Zander had leaped on the incredible hulk's back and was punching the bodyguard on the head. *Brave move, Zander, but not brilliant.* The guard shrugged him off and with one backhanded blow swatted Zander to the ground.

"Never mind them! Help me with the brothers!" ordered Dr. Halpert.

The huge man stared at Halpert. A flicker of disdain flashed in his eyes. Maybe he was tired of taking orders. Maybe he just wanted to squash bugs. He snarled and gave me a two-handed shove that propelled me into the window. My forehead cracked against the thick pane. Then, in a slow, menacing movement, the great Goliath shifted his attention to Gia. She stood waiting, knees bent, balanced on the balls of her feet. Gia calmly clasped her hands, stretched her arms toward the ceiling. She loosened her neck, tilting it from side to side.

As chill as a cucumber salad at a family picnic.

The guard didn't consider the skinny girl with purple hair a threat. He relaxed his defenses. That was a mistake. Gia delivered a lightning-swift, devastating punch to his neck. She instantly whirled and brought a whiplike roundhouse kick to his face.

The hulk toppled to the ground like a great tree felled to the forest floor. The man slowly rose, shaking the cobwebs from his head in disbelief. He flashed an amused smile. Finally, happy at last, he had found a worthy adversary.

Gia waited in ready position, bouncing on the balls of her feet, hands open.

"This isn't the time for that!" Dr. Halpert blustered. "The brothers! You must help me now!" Water still poured from the sprinkler system.

The massive man glowered at Gia. He snorted, a rhino's grunt. Then he turned sharply away and gathered up the pale, wraithlike twins in his massive arms.

Halpert called out instructions to the bodyguard over the deafening blare of alarm bells. "Carry them through the tunnels to the heliport. Move quickly! I'll initiate the file-destruct sequence from the communication center."

The sprinklers slowed to a steady drip. Zander rose groggily from the wet floor. I could see that his nose was broken. Bright red blood puddled at his feet, turning pink on the floor as it mixed with the water. "Let's go," I yelled, yanking him by the arm. I lifted up Dane to my face and kissed him. Gia advanced to the lead, and the four of us swept out of the room.

For some reason, the mansion's sound system began blasting David Bowie—*"Ch-ch-changes"*—at earsplitting volume. Until that moment, I hadn't realized that Talal Mirwani was a Bowie fan. But then again, isn't everybody?

"Turn and face the strange!"

"What happened back there?" Zander yelled as we splashed and slipped down the hallway.

"It was Talal!" I yelled over the noise. "He must have found a way to hack into the estate's mainframe!"

Dane sniffed. "I smell smoke."

"Dane's right," Gia confirmed. "It's coming from the main floor. We'd better move."

I lowered Dane from my arms to the floor. I held my brother by the shoulders to get his full attention. "Go with Gia and Zander, they'll take care of you."

"No, I want you," Dane said, clutching at my shirt.

"I'll meet you outside," I promised. "I have something to do first." I looked up at my friends. "Take him outside. Find a safe place. The fire department should be here soon."

I squeezed Dane's small body close to my chest. "I love you, Scarecrow! Now go!"

Gia lifted Dane up in her sinewy arms. He clung to her, buried his face in her neck. "I've got him," she called back. "Go do what you have to do."

I took off down the hallway. I needed to find some way to get in direct contact with Talal. There might still be a way to stop the Borks from fleeing. Halpert had mentioned a communication center. I tore down a long hallway, paused by a guard's abandoned desk, and read a sign on the door behind it: DR. NOAH HALPERT.

I tried the knob. It was unlocked.

I scanned the room. Bookshelves, chairs, a large desk. Somewhere a phone rang. I recognized the ringtone. Dr. Halpert's blue blazer, now soaking wet, lay neatly folded across a wooden armchair. I reached into the pocket and answered my cell. "Tal?"

"None other," he replied.

"There's a fire downstairs. Did you cause it?"

Tal paused before answering. I could hear the clicking of a computer keyboard. "No, that must have been Halpert. They don't want to leave behind any evidence."

"Can you put it out?" I asked.

"I can try, no promises. I gained control of most of their operating systems, but they don't have sprinklers at every level. Fires are not easy to tame—they have a way of going wherever they want. You'd better hurry," he said. "The police are on the way. Fire department, too."

"The Borks are headed for the heliport," I said. "See if you can stop them, or delay them, or whatever!"

"I'm already on it," Talal said, and I could almost hear him smile through the phone.

"I'm headed there now," I told him. I shoved the phone into my pocket, ran three steps, and stopped in my tracks. I picked up the phone. "Tal?"

"Yeah?"

"Which way to the heliport?"

He told me.

Next I ran down the hall, down two flights of stairs, pushed through three sets of heavy metal double doors, crossed an open yard, and arrived at a barnlike structure. *Clack, clack, clack*—tumblers turned, locks released, doors swung open before me.

Tal was clearing my path.

The barn was empty. Two huge sliding doors had been left wide open.

A siren wailed in the distance, growing louder.

My phone rang.

"Yeah?"

It was Tal. "Sorry, but Elvis has left the building."

An involuntary noise rose up from inside me, something between a gasp and a groan. A helicopter lifted off from behind a stand of tall pines. It hovered for a moment, tilted away, and disappeared. The Borks had made their getaway.

No one would believe our story now.

I spoke into the cell. "Thanks for everything, Tal. You saved us. I'll never make fun of computer geeks again." I paused, almost afraid to ask. "Is Dane okay? Gia? Zander?"

"Safe and sound, wet and shivering, but with wool blankets wrapped around their shoulders," Talal answered. "The first responders have arrived: cops, EMTs, firefighters, even the sheriff's office. It's all clear. You might want to say hello."

BY THE CLEAR MORNING LIGHT

I slept hard that night, and dreamlessly, as if I'd fallen down a watery well. By the clear morning light, I awoke refreshed, renewed. Dane was on the floor in the TV room, organizing his Halloween loot. "Wanna trade?" he asked, before even saying hello.

"You got any Jolly Ranchers?"

Dane scanned his ridiculous stash. "Seventeen pieces," he informed me.

"What are you looking for in exchange?"

"Kit Kats or peanut butter cups," he said. "And Mounds bars for Mom. She likes coconut, no one knows why."

The kid cracked me up. "I think we can work something out," I said. "Later, okay? I have to stop by the school."

"It's Sunday."

"I know," I said. "Zander's already there. Gia, too. We're helping out in the garden."

"Dorothy's super strong," Dane noted.

"You mean Gia? Yeah, she sure is," I agreed, still awed by her fighting skills. I recalled that famous quote from the boxer Muhammad Ali: *Float like a butterfly, sting like a bee.*

That was Gia all right.

I eased myself down onto the edge of a chair and softly asked, "Hey, Dane. You okay about last night?"

Dane beamed. "It rained inside the house!"

I laughed. "That was pretty crazy weather, huh?"

"It was just like in the movie," Dane said, "when

we all had to be brave. In the end, the Wizard wasn't so powerful after all."

"Promise me you'll never again get into a stranger's car," I said. "We won't tell Mom about that, okay?"

Dane had to think about that one. "Secrets are bad."

It was my turn to think it over. "You're probably right. If you want to tell Mom, let's do it together, okay? We don't want to worry her too much."

Dane tossed me a green Jolly Rancher.

"Thanks, brother," I said. "I owe you."

The world might have gone wrong in so many ways, but it still looked good to me as I pedaled to the middle school. The bee frame was back up. Ms. Fjord worked close to it, fully dressed in a beekeeper's protective outfit. She waved a small container that blew smoke over the hive.

Gia and Zander stood nearby. Zander wore a white bandage over his nose, with two white strips in the shape of an X. "Ouch," I said.

Zander shrugged. His eyes darted to Ms. Fjord,

and he said, a little too loudly, "Clumsy me, broke my nose last night."

"He walked into a door," Gia explained.

"Uh-huh," I said. "Does it hurt?"

"Only if I breathe," Zander joked. He gently probed the blackened and bruised area of his nose.

Ms. Fjord joined us, lifting off the head veil.

"So how's the colony?" I asked.

"We got lucky," she replied, stepping back to observe the restored frame. "This morning I used a smoker to calm them down. Then, with the help of your friends, I replaced a couple of supers and the outer cover, so the frame itself is now structurally sound. It's late in the season, so there wasn't much honey to speak of. Otherwise, it would have been a gooey mess. My big worry was the health of the queen."

Zander interjected, "Without a queen, a colony can't survive. She's the heart and soul of the hive."

"And?" I asked.

"She appears fine, for now," Ms. Fjord answered. "I might have to replace her with another queen, preferably in the spring. Queens only last two or three years, and it's essential that she be a productive queen. Everything in the hive revolves around her."

Images from last night scrolled before me: the shock of seeing the powerful Borks in their crisp blue pajamas, sick and still bound together, brothers sharing one flawed, dark heart; the water gushing from the sprinklers; Gia's roundhouse kick; Dane in my arms; and the sight of a helicopter's blades slicing through the dark clouds.

A feeling that it was over, for now.

"What happens when bees swarm?" Gia asked, breaking my reverie.

Ms. Fjord rubbed her brow with the back of her sleeve. "Well, let's see," she said. "A hive will typically swarm if there's a problem in the colony, often because it's too crowded or too hot, or if there's a problem with the queen. A swarm is a fascinating natural event to witness," she said. "The hive suddenly gets really loud, and thousands of bees rise up at once, like a swirling black tornado. They fly off to gather in a great clump, hanging off a nearby tree branch or bush. Keepers call them beards."

"Beards?" I said.

"Oh, it's incredible, just a great big dangling mass of bees! They'll hang there for a full day or two while scouts go out in all directions to seek a new location for the colony. It could be a chimney, a hole in a tree, any kind of small, dark place."

"There're lots of great videos online," Zander suggested. "You should check them out."

"I almost forgot, Zander," Ms. Fjord said, tapping the side of her head to signal forgetfulness. "I received some great news yesterday about your application. It's not official yet, but a friend of mine on the committee told me that you've been selected as the winner of the Young Beekeeper Award."

"What? Really?!" An enormous smile was plastered across Zander's bandaged face. He impulsively hugged Ms. Fjord, almost lifting her off the ground. "Thank you, thank you!"

"It wasn't me," she said, laughing. "It was you, Zander. You did all the work—you deserve it. I'm so proud of you. And I'm happy for the honeybees, too."

"Looks like you'll have your own hive soon," Gia said to Zander, patting his back. "As long as there are people like you around, the honeybees have a chance."

"Yes," I added, "but no Twizzler is safe."

GIA

We'd hiked for an hour when I paused, sniffing the air. My sense of smell was back. I leaned against a rock, unshouldered my pack, and pulled out a water bottle. "Want some?" I asked Gia.

She took it and drank deeply.

"How much did you know?" I asked her.

She handed the bottle back to me, raised a quizzical eyebrow.

"You know what I mean," I said. "The fight outside Leo's, the train derailment, even hiring Talal in the first place. You know things before they happen."

Gia shrugged. "It's hard to explain."

"Try," I said.

"I always loved nature." She leaned back and opened her arms wide. "It's always been my happy place, ever since I was a little girl. But that day with the bees, when I got stung so many times . . .

"Something in me changed that day."

She fell silent, head tilted to the ground. After a long pause, she looked back up at me. "Sometimes I can feel events coming together. Most aspects about the future are blank, just darkness and silence. It's not like I can predict when we're going to have a math quiz."

"What about me?"

"You?" Gia smiled. "I could foresee our paths converging. Maybe that's just a girl thing."

"Intuition," I said.

Gia smiled. "Like the queen bee said, *it all connects.*"

I looked around. We were on a loop trail in a small forest preserve. I'd never been to this place before, though it was only a long bike ride from my house. Maybe Gia knew where we were going all along—I couldn't be sure.

"Gia Demeter," I said. "That's an interesting name."

"I'm glad you think so."

I said, "Demeter is a name in Greek mythology—she's a goddess of the earth. She created winter, or so the story goes, by grieving the absence of her daughter, Persephone."

"You've done your homework," Gia said. "It was also said that she had the power to give life after death to those who learn her mysteries."

"The name Gia threw me," I said. "Then I stumbled upon Gaia, the great mother of all, according to Greek myth."

"Interesting," Gia said. She took another swig of water.

"You like this place, don't you?"

"I love it," she answered, raising her eyes to take in the tall trees. "I feel connected to the earth in a deep way."

"I can see that."

She sat beside me on the rock. "The Japanese have an expression, *shinrin-yoku*. It means 'forest bathing.' I believe in it."

"Like sunbathing?"

"Exactly," she said. "The idea is that it's healthy to spend time in the forest, surrounded by the natural world. Forests are magical places."

Two birds swooped overhead, darting into the branches. Not drones, not spies, but real birds.

"Cave swallows, I think," Gia identified them, again seeming to read my thoughts. "Not from around here, but climate change affects us all."

"I wish I knew you before . . . you know, this."

"Before you died?" Gia asked.

I nodded, looking away. "This isn't who I really am."

Gia laughed, one short burst: "*Ha!* That's ridiculous, Adrian. Nobody knows who they really are! It's a journey. We discover ourselves along the way."

"Yeah, but . . ."

"Nature adapts," Gia said. "Nature survives. The

earth is something worth fighting for, just like you."

"Thanks," I said, hoisting up my pack. "You ready?"

"Almost," Gia said.

She placed her hand on my chest, leaned in, and pressed her lips to mine.

"Sweet Adrian," she said.

I felt the sting from her fingertips. A short, sharp injection, followed by a tingling sensation. Blood pumping in and out, in and out.

Tu-tump, tu-tump, tu-tump.

A magical thrum.

My heartbeat.

ACKNOWLEDGMENTS

Special thanks to Jen Ford—for help with the bees. And to my oldest son, Nicholas, who read and commented and cautioned me throughout the process. The fine work of Bill McKibben, both in his writing and in his activism, has long been an inspiration and source of light. And to my editor, Liz Szabla, who let this book happen in its own sweet, agonizing time. I began taking notes, writing scenes, and sketching character studies back in 2010. Liz has encouraged me unfailingly throughout, including during the long silences of rumination and self-doubt. This book doesn't happen without Liz.

Thank you for reading this Feiwel and Friends book.
The Friends who made

BETTER OFF unDEAD

possible are:

JEAN FEIWEL, Publisher

LIZ SZABLA, Associate Publisher

RICH DEAS, Senior Creative Director

HOLLY WEST, Editor

ALEXEI ESIKOFF, Senior Managing Editor

RAYMOND ERNESTO COLÓN, Production Manager

ANNA ROBERTO, Editor

CHRISTINE BARCELLONA, Associate Editor

KAT BRZOZOWSKI, Editor

ANNA POON, Assistant Editor

EMILY SETTLE, Administrative Assistant

STARR BAER, Production Editor

CAROL LY, Designer